# BITTEN IN THE MIDLIFE

## FANGED AFTER FORTY, BOOK 1

LIA DAVIS

L.A. BORUFF

Bitten in the Midlife

Published by Davis Raynes Publishing

PO Box 224

Middleburg, FL 32050

DavisRaynesPublishing.com

Cover by Glowing Moon Designs

Formatting by Glowing Moon Designs

DavisRaynesPublishing.com

FANGED AFTER FORTY

Fanged After Forty is a new witty spin-off from the bestselling series Witching After Forty about a forty year old nurse who moves to Philly after being left at the alter on her wedding day. The move and fresh start becomes more than Hailey Whitfield bargained for.

Now she is forty and fanged and took on a new career, Bounty Hunting.

**Reading Order:**
Bitten in the Midlife
Staked in the Midlife
Masquerading in the Midlife
Many more adventures to come...

BITTEN IN THE MIDLIFE
FANGED AFTER FORTY, BOOK 1

Jilted at the altar a month before her fortieth birthday. Poor Hailey. Midlife really does have a crisis. Or is it that midlife *is* the crisis? Either way, it sucks.

Hailey Whitfield can't take anymore run-ins with her ex. It's time for a big change.

She's never considered moving away, but it's her best plan yet. Bonus – her bestie lives next door! However, her new neighbor is... weird, to say the least. *Extremely* hot, but odd. So are his friends. But Hailey will take strange neighbors over facing her lying, cheat, deadbeat ex-fiancé all day, any day.

Finding a job in a new town is more challenging than she realizes. With her savings depleted from the move, Hailey has to suck it up and take what she gets. After taking a job as a private nurse for an injured bounty hunter, things start to look up.

Then a skip falls into her lap. Okay, sure. She was being nosy and reading an incoming fax intended for her patient. But with a little encouragement, Hailey takes on the task of tracking down the skip.

It's easy money. Right?

Wrong. This skip is far more than Hailey bargained for. And her life is about to change in a very bloody and pointy kind of way. What a bite in the... Well, you know.

With the help of her witchy best friend and her new, very pale neighbor, Hailey is going to collect her bounty.

Or die trying.

## CHAPTER ONE

The day had finally come, and I could hardly contain my excitement.

I never knew starting over at the not-so-ripe age of forty would be so freeing. It was like a huge weight lifted off my whole body. I was *free*!

I didn't have to look at my ex-fiancé's face anymore. Nor did I have to watch him openly flirt with all the other nurses. I didn't have to watch him happily move on to the tramp he cheated on me with.

Jerk.

He was a lot more than a jerk, but I was *not* thinking about him anymore. Plus, karma always got back at the people who deserved her wrath. I was starting my new life in a new city, in my new-to-me house.

The best part of this move was that my neighbor was my best friend since we were in diapers.

We were celebrating this glorious day with champagne on my front porch, ogling the movers as they unloaded the truck and carried all of my things into the house.

It was a great way to celebrate on a Monday.

See? Not all Mondays were bad.

Another thing that made this move better for my sanity was that I was closer to my two older brothers. One I adored, Luke. The other was the eldest of the five of us, and...the poor guy wasn't everyone's favorite. We all loved him, but we wouldn't walk out in front of a bus to save him. Oliver was just...Oliver. He was a hard person to figure out. Oh, calm down. We'd save him. We might just shove him out of the way extra hard.

Pushing away thoughts of family and ex-jerkface, I went back to supervising the movers. It was a tough job, but someone had to do it.

"What about that one?" Kendra asked, pointing at one of the moving guys.

I hid my smile behind the crystal champagne flute she had brought with her.

My bestie had taken the day off to celebrate with me. She was a lawyer and had just won a big case, so that gave us double the reasons to celebrate.

Good times!

I watched mister tall, blond, and delicious—with rippling abs, a luscious tush I could've bounced a quarter off of, and one of those cute little man buns—carry a large box toward us.

He was young enough to call me mama, but still legal. Maybe being a cougar wasn't such a bad idea, just as long as he left before the sun was up. I had no plans to wake up beside another man, ever.

Did you hear me? *Ever*.

It would give my eldest brother, Oliver, something else to turn his nose up at and lecture me about why it wasn't a good idea to date a man young enough to be my son.

At least Luke would support a fling with the hot moving man. On second thought, Luke supported orgies and any manner of sexual escapades. That was a little too many hands, arms, legs, and bodies for me.

No, thank you. Although... maybe... Nope.

As the cutie with the man bun walked past, he batted a pair of lashes that looked like someone had dipped them in chocolate, and I glanced down at his pants, totally by accident.

No, really. I didn't mean to.

But oh, my. His pants fit like they'd been painted on. Molded to every muscle of his body, but also like they were begging to be torn off. It'd been a while since I'd had a back to rake my fingernails down.

Kendra, my bestie for as long as I could remember, cocked a dark brow, then shrugged. "I have socks older than he is."

I snorted, then giggled. It was probably the champagne, but who cared. "I didn't say I wanted to marry him."

God forbid. One bite of that sour apple was enough for me, and even if spitting out that second bite wasn't my choice, I was over the whole idea. Kendra had it right. Her love 'em and leave 'em lifestyle was my inspiration from now on. New start, new motto.

Broken hearts were a young woman's game, and I wasn't young enough to be willing to risk another. No way, buddy.

"Since when is a little bump and grind enough for you?" Skeptical was Kendra's middle name, while a smile flirted with her lips. Her skeptical part sure helped in her budding law career. Her last name was Justice, after all. Literally.

Kendra didn't trust easily, which was why she'd

4

stayed single after her divorce almost fifteen years ago.

I shrugged and watched a mover lean against a dolly full of boxes while he rode the truck gate to the ground. Shirtless, muscular, and blond were apparently my new turn-on. Who knew I had a type? "Being ditched at the altar was eye-opening and threw my entire life in a new direction," I mumbled.

This direction's sheen of sweat, when combined with the champagne, put thoughts into my head. Fun thoughts. Sexy thoughts. Thoughts a newly single woman with no prospects had no business having— or maybe every business having them.

The best part was I didn't have to wake up next to anyone or answer to anyone. Ever. Again.

"Have you found a job yet?" It figured Kendra would change the subject to something more serious... What a way to snap me back to reality.

She was such a buzzkill sometimes.

"No, but I put in applications and sent copies of my résumé out to hospitals within fifty miles as well as every doctor's office in the greater Chestnut Hill-Philadelphia area. I also found an agency offering private nursing that I'm thinking of checking out." At this point, I had to take what I could get. My life savings had gone into the sanity-saving move.

Kendra nodded. Her approval wasn't essential, but the validation was nice. "Have you met the neighbors yet?"

She knew I'd come to tour the house and talk to the previous owner about a week ago. Kendra had been on some witch's retreat at the time.

Pointing to the house on the other side of mine, she said, "Sara lives there with her two-point-five kids and a husband who is never home. She's nice, but on the snobbish side. She is one hundred percent human, like you. Don't tell her anything you don't want the whole neighborhood to know."

Kendra had connections with the neighborhood I didn't, yet. There were two reasons for those connections. One, she was a witch; Two, she'd lived in this neighborhood for the past fifteen years. She'd moved right after her divorce to start a new life with her kids. Of course, she now had a great relationship with her ex. They made better friends than lovers, as it turned out.

It had been the same years ago for me and my ex-husband, Howard Jefferies. Our divorce had been messy and painful, mostly because I hadn't wanted to admit we'd fallen out of love with each other. I was bitter for a long time before we'd finally become friends.

"No. I've been here a couple of times, but always during the day when people are working, I suppose." I hadn't met a single soul besides the previous owner, Ava Harper, who was also a witch, and her extended family that had been with her.

Kendra hid her smile with another drink. "The neighbors across the street are," she leaned closer to me and lowered her voice, "*weird.*"

"Yeah?" I glanced at the house across the street. "How so?"

It was a large three-story, modern brick house with a balcony that wrapped around the top floor. I wondered if the top floor was one large room or a separate apartment or living space.

Black shutters accented the windows, which appeared to be blacked out. The front door was crimson with black gothic-looking embellishments. There was a front porch on the ground level that was half the length of the front of the house, and the lawn was perfectly manicured with lush green grass and expertly trimmed bushes.

"You know, *weird.*" Kendra cocked an eyebrow. "*My* kind of weird."

Maybe she'd had too much to drink, or I had, because I wasn't following whatever it was she hinted at. Then it hit me. Oh! *Her* kind of weird.

"You mean like..." I lowered my voice to a whisper as I looked around to make sure there wasn't anyone in earshot. "Witches?"

She shook her head, and I pursed my lips. A guessing game. Awesome. I *so* sucked at those.

I kept my voice low enough that only the two of us could hear. "You said there's more than witches out there. Is it one of the others?"

This time, she tapped the left side of her nose and smiled. Kendra so loved her dramatics.

"Werewolves?"

"No."

"Werepanthers?"

"Nope."

"Bears?" I paused for another negative reply, then ran through a list. "Dragons? Lions? Cats of any kind?"

"No, no, and no." She kept her brow cocked and her smirk in place. She loved torturing me with these crazy guess games.

"Llama, dog, sock puppet?"

She burst out laughing at the latter, drawing glances from the movers. We laughed together like old times. Being around Kendra was soothing after everything I'd been through. God, I'd missed her so much.

"If we were playing the hot-cold game, I would say you were getting hot, but you're very cold." That helped so much. Not. Cryptic hints were her thing. "Brr." She ran her hands over her arms and faked a shiver. Then cackled like the witch she was.

"Zombies? Something in the abominable category?" Now I was reaching into the tundra. While Philly was cold in the winter, anything of the snow critter variety wouldn't stand a chance in a Pennsylvania summer.

"Warmer with zombies, a little too cold with the snowman."

My tone dropped to reflect my almost boredom. "Ghoul? Ghost? Alien?" She was losing me.

"Oh, come on!" She stood to her full height and leaned against the rail on the porch to stare at me. "You're dancing right around it." She let her tongue slip over her canine.

Oh, snap! No way.

"Vampire?" I whispered that one, too, because I'd read somewhere that vamps could hear every pin drop in a five-mile radius. Then again, that article was on the internet, and you couldn't trust anything on the web. At least I didn't.

I stared at the house again after her wink, indicating that I guessed right. Finally, the gothic embellishments and blacked-out windows now made a little more sense. However, the home looked normal at the same time.

"Wow." Were they friendly vampires?

"Yeah." She nodded with her lips pursed.

We both shifted to look at the truck, right as one of my boxes went crashing to the ground and the sound of breaking glass tinkled through the air.

I groaned inwardly and hoped there wasn't something valuable in that box. The movers would be getting a bill for it if it was.

Later, after the hotties had left and the sun began to set, Kendra started unpacking the kitchen while I worked in the living room. Thank goodness they'd put the boxes in the rooms they belonged in, thanks to my OCD in labeling each one.

I was knee-deep in opened boxes and bubble wrap when the doorbell rang. "I'll get it," I called in Kendra in the kitchen.

Not waiting for her to answer, I swung the door open and froze.

The most exquisite man I'd ever seen stood in the doorway.

Hellooooo handsome.

This guy was...tall. Well, taller than my five-one height, but then, most people were. He towered over me with a lean, athletic rather than muscular form. His deep amber eyes reminded me of a sunset, while his pale skin said he didn't spend much time in the sun. Light hair, something in the blond to strawberry range, brushed the tops of his shoulders. Shiny, clean, and begging for my fingers to run through the strands.

Smiling as if he could read my mind, Strawberry Man handed me a basket smelling strongly of blueberry muffins. The smell made my mouth water. Or was that him? Maybe he was Blueberry Man... Oh, geez. I hadn't even said a word yet. Had I?

"These are for you." He nodded toward the basket, looking a little uncomfortable.

Oh, yes, they were. His large hand brushed mine as I grabbed it, and I sucked in a short, quick breath. At some point, I'd become awkward. And ridiculous.

I remembered I hadn't brushed my hair all day since the movers arrived. Damn.

The porch was smaller with him standing on it, somehow it had shrunk, and I couldn't draw in a breath around him. Dramatic, yes, but so true. Or maybe he was too hot, and all the oxygen had evaporated in his presence. Either way, I found it hard to breathe and think.

"Um, th-thank you." I was like a nervous

teenager who'd just met her very first pretty boy. I chuckled, hiccupped, and would've fallen out the door if not for the doorframe I'd somehow managed to catch my shirt on.

He nodded, smiling as he tilted his head. Damn if my knees didn't go weak. "No problem. If you need anything at all, I'm Jaxon. Uh, Jax, and I live right over there." He pointed to the house across the street. The back view of his head made my heart pitter-patter and my belly rumble as much as the front of him did.

"You're the..." I didn't know if he, if they, were loud and proud with their creatures of the night status, and I didn't want to take the chance of outing Kendra for telling me. Unfortunately, I thought of it a second *after* I'd started speaking. "Neighbor."

His grin hit me like sunshine poking through the clouds on a rainy day. Ironic, since vampire meant allergic to the sun in a deadly kind of way.

"Yeah."

I didn't know if I should invite him in. What if there was a Mrs. Vampire? The last thing I needed was to become a jealous vampire wife's main course.

Like the queen of the dorks, I held up the basket, gave it a sniff, then hiccupped again. "Thanks for the goodies." I wasn't usually so awkward. There was something about this guy.

As I spoke, I wished again I'd taken a moment to brush my hair or put on a clean shirt before I answered the door. Vampire or not, this guy deserved a neighbor who combed her hair.

CHAPTER TWO

Tuesday came in like a lion with a couple of bites on the message board where I'd posted for jobs in private nursing. And bingo!

One, if they hired me, they needed me to start immediately. Hope bloomed in my chest and for once, I didn't tamp it down. I didn't tell myself this wasn't going to happen. I was an optimist. Newly formed, but enthused and excited.

This was my break. Because this girl was *broke*.

Calming myself just a little, I typed a reply to the sender. **I would be happy to discuss the position at your earliest convenience.**

It sounded formal enough. I hoped.

She replied quickly. **Is now too soon?** The

sender added an address and my heart leaped. One day in town, and I was on my way to an interview.

**I can be there in thirty minutes.**

Because I wasn't a complete bumbling idiot, I didn't tell her I'd already showered and would only need to change into something that didn't say I had planned to spend the day unpacking boxes. I was an early riser, always had been. A morning person, to the disgust of both my exes.

After changing clothes, I was in the car on my way to the Chestnut Apartments. Thank goodness for GPS. I was too nervous to find my way, and with my luck, I would've ended up in Jersey rather than Center City West in Philly.

Center City was the wealthy section of the city. At least, this apartment building was. Glass and metal and windows all the way around. The views of the city alone sold the place.

After checking in with the front desk, I was sent right up to the apartment. She must have been expecting me because the door opened before I could knock.

"Hello, I'm Tracy. You must be Hailey." The woman had long black hair and dark brown eyes. "Thank you for coming."

We shook hands, then she led me into the apartment. As I'd thought before entering the building, I could see for miles out of the floor-to-ceiling windows in the living room. The location was one of those to die for, close to everything, like my brother Luke's gallery, for example.

Tracy moved into the kitchen area, which was separated by a small island, so I followed, taking note of the large open space of the apartment and the small nook up against the wall of glass. The counter-tops were black and silver marble. White cabinets lined up under and above the counter; The appliances were stainless steel. Everything was luxurious.

When she had two cups of steaming tea poured, we sat at the nook. "Cleo is my mother. She's a fifty-five-year-old bounty hunter, who probably should've stopped the stakeouts and takedowns a few years ago, but she claims to love what she does." She sighed. "And, admittedly, she was a pretty badass bounty hunter. She put hunters half her age to shame. But bullets don't care how badass you are."

Tracy shrugged and whipped her hair over her shoulder. "Her last hunt, a few weeks ago, the perp—you'll get used to Mom's lingo—anyway, the perp pulled a gun and shot her. The bullet grazed her spine." She shuddered, closed her eyes, then opened them again after a few seconds and one long exhale.

"It's going to take a while before she's back on her feet, much less hunting down perps and hauling them in."

I nodded. Tracy spoke about a thousand words a minute, as if there was a premium on how much she could say at one time. "All right."

"She needs round-the-clock care, so we've broken it up into three shifts. There's morning until early afternoon, early afternoon until mid-evening, then a bedtime shift." She outlined the pay, and it wasn't nearly what I expected, but at least I wouldn't have to go asking for handouts from any of my family.

Oliver was a hard no. He was stingy with his money and often blamed his kids and wife for spending it all. My sisters never had any money. Luke had plenty and would give me a little to help make it through tough times, but I didn't want to ask him.

This job would help pay the bills. I'll just go without cable and only eat every other day. No biggie.

After a brief silence, Tracy added, "I've moved back in temporarily until she gets back on her feet, but I work full time, *and* I'm taking classes to get my master's degree."

Sheesh. Busy woman. Tracy asked all the usual

interview questions. Reliable transportation? If necessary, could I stay later or come in early? What shift would I prefer?

"Day shifts." I was wide open for availability, but I liked mornings. Even when I was young, I'd enjoyed getting up early and feeling the morning sun on my face. I could get a lot of stuff done before noon.

"Excellent. The other girls are still in school; they want to split the evenings and bedtime shifts, so this is perfect." Tracy smiled like some great weight had been lifted from her shoulders. I imagined it had been. I'd seen many sick mothers in the years since I started working in the medical field. The worry alone when someone else provided the care was enough to turn a young woman old. Tracy was smart to get help.

I signed the papers authorizing the background check, and Tracy smiled. "This should just take a day or two then I'll give you a call and you can get started by the time Mom is home from the hospital."

I nodded and shook her hand again on my way out.

It was a beautiful, unseasonably warm March day, and instead of driving and having to deal with Philly parking, I left my car in the underground parking garage at the apartments and walked the few blocks to Luke's gallery.

When I arrived, my brother was in mid-conversation with a client, but he stopped talking and a wide grin spread across his face when he noticed me. "Girl*friend*!" His extra emphasis on friend made me laugh. "What are you doing here?" He toe-ran across the space and air-kissed me on each side of my face. "You look fab! What brings you so close to the action?"

"Job interview," I said. Luke's perfectly coiffed hair and Armani suit gave him the air of a man with money, a man with style, and a man with his own personal shopper. All of these things were true. The personal shopper was his new boy toy, Favio. I suspected Favio wasn't his real name, but since it wasn't a detail that mattered, I went on liking him all the same.

Luke adjusted an invisible out of place hair from his forehead with the daintiest of fingers, then smiled and cocked his head. "Let me get rid of this art enthusiast," he leaned in and whispered, rolling his eyes. I didn't have to guess that the client had zero art intelligence. "Then I'll take you to lunch."

Lunch sounded fabulous. It had been a while

since we'd had a chance to sit down and catch up. I browsed until Luke was ready to go.

Of all my brothers and sisters, I saw Luke the most. Oliver never took a day off, never left his office, and from nine to six, Monday through Friday, he was off-limits. But after work, when the sun went down, Ollie knew how to get down. In his younger days, anyway. I didn't know about it, now. He'd just turned forty-five and it had hit him hard. Something about his mortality staring him in the face, he'd said. My sisters told me he was a different man, though just as hard-nosed. I hadn't talked to Ollie much in recent years. I just couldn't face the judgment of being emotionally close to him, so I'd put some distance between us quite a while ago.

"Have you talked to the girls?" I asked when we started down the sidewalk toward his favorite bistro-style restaurant.

He sighed. Luke was the hub of all familial information for the Whitfield clan. Then he distributed the gossip among each of us. "Ally called me yesterday." Allison and Avery were the twins, our mom's late-in-life children with our dad. Her *special* surprises. At twenty-six, they lived in New York and acted on Broadway. They both had quite the flair for the dramatic, and I never really knew if it was because they were the youngest or if they had some special skill.

"And?" He was building anticipation, withholding the information until I asked. The girls weren't the only ones with dramatic tendencies.

"They got a commercial, toothpaste of all things." He widened his eyes at me. "And Ollie is, of course, chomping at the bit to invest their income so they can shelter from taxes or something." He slapped a hand through the air. "Such a pain in my surgically enhanced backside. And his wife..." As well as a trophy wife, Ollie had the requisite son and daughter who attended private school and knew to hold out their pinkies when they sipped tea at the country club. As a bonus for all of us, he had an opinion he loved to share about every single thing. Everything. I'm whispering now. *Everything*.

"What about her?" Luke hated Victoria Beckett-Whitfield. In my opinion, he hated that she got a hyphenated last name, and he didn't, but I'd never voiced that concern.

"Bun in her oven." He cocked his head. "That tummy tuck? *Worth-less*." He sing-songed the last word like it gave him pleasure to say it.

"You're so bad." Not really, and I loved him no matter what anyway.

"Yet you love me." He leaned in and air-kissed me again.

Once we sat down and gave our orders, I changed the subject. "How are things with Favio?" While Luke loved to gossip, there was nothing he liked more than talking about himself.

"O-ver." He double thumbs-downed, then faked-swiped away a tear. "He was using me for my money, my apartment, and of course my skills in the boudoir." His grimace was the punctuation for his sentence. "I'm single and on the mingle. So, if you find something luscious of the tall, dark, and delicious variety, send him my way."

I laughed. Where the hell was I going to meet anyone of the delicious variety? Well, except my new nightwalker neighbor. Now that was one delicious specimen of a man. Erm, vampire. Still man. No way was I telling Luke about him yet. No point in freaking out the family over a guy who hadn't even looked my way.

Not that I was considering dating a vampire. Maybe a nice tumble under the sheets. But nothing long-term. Not going down that road again.

Ever. Have I mentioned that yet? Never.

"Of course," I agreed, and took a drink of my soda.

"Anything from Brad?" His eyes narrowed, and his face contorted every time he asked about my ex.

I rolled my eyes. "Nothing more than the usual BS. He loves me, misses me. He's so sorry he broke my heart. Sent me flowers." I hadn't even read the card. I would have thrown the flowers in the trash, but they were my favorite—pink roses. So as long as I pretended someone else gave them to me, they stayed.

"Ugh." An actual shocking sound was a few rungs beneath Luke, but he tried, and I appreciated the effort. "I thought he moved on with some nurse from the hospital?" he asked.

I shrugged. "I'm not sure if he's just apologizing and trying to calm his guilt, or if she left him and he's trying to get back with me. Either way, I'm not interested."

Luke snarled his upper lip. "He was so not good enough for you."

It had taken a while for me to realize that, but I finally agreed. "I'm just glad he's gone."

Luke nodded. "Well, if you need help keeping him gone, you let me know."

"Aww, is my big brother going to kick my bad ex-fiancé's ass for me?" The idea was laughable. Probably why Luke laughed.

He held out his hand. "Absolutely not. My manicurist would kick *my* ass. I will happily pay someone to show the man who left my sister at the altar the business end of a knuckle sandwich." He grinned and put up his fists like he was going to fight, then pulled his fists in front of his face and blew his nails as if he was drying the clear polish he kept on them.

We spent the rest of lunch with gossip and laughter. Luke, with his creamy skin and blond-blue beauty, was the social darling of the family, and there was no one I would rather have celebrated my new job with.

CHAPTER THREE

By the time I'd gotten back from having lunch with Luke yesterday, I'd received a text saying that my background check came back, Cleo was being discharged from the hospital this morning, and Tracy wanted me there bright and early. So naturally, I was wide awake at 5:00 a.m., but didn't need to be there until eight.

You could say I was a tad excited. Or was it anxious? It was probably both.

I wasn't surprised that the background check came back so fast. My record was squeaky clean. Although, it had been really hard not to tarnish that record many times while working with Brad the jerkface. So, this move didn't only save my sanity, but helped keep my perfect record clean. It was the one time in my life that having no life had paid off.

I was two minutes early for the first day of my new job. I didn't want to be too early, and I didn't want to be late. Did I mention I had a touch of OCD? Yeah, well, I did.

Tracy opened the door and smiled with a bit of relief in her features. She just didn't know how badly I needed this job. "Thank you for coming."

"I should be thanking you for hiring me." Oh, great, that sounded desperate. Well, I was getting there.

After shutting the door, she led me down the short hall into the living room/kitchen combo. I was drawn to the wall of glass overlooking the city, just like I had been the other day during my interview. The view was incredible.

Tracy gave me a short tour of the apartment. The bedroom adjacent to the living room was converted into Cleo's office. The master bedroom was the first right just before entering the living room.

"Mom is asleep now or I'd introduce you, but she's generally pretty awake and alert and she can tell you where to find things." Tracy gathered her books from the various tables in the rooms. During the interview, she'd told me she went back to school to get her master's in criminal defense. "Her medicine schedule is on the fridge, and she loves to try to distract you from making her take them." She chuckled. "She says they make her ditzy."

"I've had plenty of experience in getting patients to take their meds. They used to say I could talk them into anything." I chuckled and shoved my hands into the pockets of my scrubs.

"Also, she likes to order food delivered." I nodded as Tracy kept rattling off things. I wondered if I needed to write all this down. If so, I was unprepared. "You don't have to clean. I'll run the vacuum and straighten up when I get home. Mom is particular about her rugs." She stopped at the door and faced me. "That's all I can think of. My number is by the medicine schedule on the fridge if you need anything."

She waved and left. I shut the door behind her and headed to the living room. A few seconds later, before I'd even had time to turn around, she came back in again and grabbed a jacket. Yesterday was warm, today was cooler. Tomorrow, there would probably be a snowman next to the Rocky statue at the art museum.

You just didn't know what the weather was going to be like.

I chuckled at my thoughts, then went into the bedroom to check on Cleo and officially meet my patient. I poked my head in the door first. She was stocky with dark skin and black hair. When she looked at me, she smiled a welcoming, open grin. "Hello. You must be Hailey."

"Yes, ma'am. You must be Cleo."

That was obvious, but I was nervous and excited to have a job. I was such a goof sometimes.

"The one and only." She let out a soft laugh. "I'm sure my daughter has told you what a difficult patient I am, but I have promised to be on my best behavior." She held up three fingers on her right hand then winced as she shifted and tried to use her free arm to push herself higher. "Mm." Her eyes squeezed shut then flipped open a moment later. "Come. Sit down. Let's chat." She was the boss. I liked her instantly. "Tell me what brings you to my neck of the woods, other than the promise of a paycheck."

Direct. I did like her already.

"Oh, where to begin." My life up to this point was a mess. Mostly. That was why I needed a reboot in a new city.

She nodded. "I knew there was a story there."

"Two stories. Husband number one was my first

big relationship. Howard and I fell in love in high school. Then somewhere in the ten years we were married, we fell *out* of love. I didn't even realize it until he pointed it out and served me with divorce papers." I shrugged and sat down in an armchair next to her bed.

Cleo frowned. "Ouch. What a jerk."

"That was my thought at the time. It took me a long time to get over it and trust that not everyone will just up and leave me." I smoothed a nonexistent wrinkle from my scrub pants.

"Anyway, I came to realize that he was right. I don't think we were actually in love. At least not deep love." I scrunched up my nose and met her gaze. "Does that make sense?"

She nodded. "It does. Tracy's dad and I were like that. Only it was me to point it out. He still tries to convince me to give it another go." Cleo picked up a glass of water from the nightstand. "Not happening. I have a rule I've never broken. If I was married to him once, there would be no second time."

"That's a good rule to have." I relaxed in my chair and crossed my legs. "Howard is a good guy when he wants to be. By happy coincidence, he was a bounty hunter, too. I helped him on occasion, so I know the ins and out of the business."

How had I forgotten the adventure, the fun we'd had? "We worked well together. Until he dropped the bomb that it was over. That was the most painful and messiest time of my life, but we've mended fences and we speak now. We found out we were better friends than a couple."

She laughed. "Bounty hunters are a hard lot. Some love their jobs more than their families. Maybe he was protecting you by getting the divorce."

Wasn't that just the truth, whole truth, and nothing but the truth? "That's what I thought too. It's all water under the bridge now. He's a good man, we met at the wrong time, wrong place, wrong life. It happens."

We laughed and shared a brief silent moment before she asked, "You said *husband number one* like there's a number two?"

"An *almost* number two." The mental picture caused an ache in my gut. I still wasn't over that one. "Brad." Even saying his name brought a wave of darkness rumbling through me. "He's a doctor at the hospital where I used to work. The SOB left me at the altar. Literally. He apparently wasn't done fishing, if you know what I mean. So, this is my new start. I needed to get away from seeing him and the fish he was screwing on our wedding day."

"Reasons to leave don't get much better than that one." Cleo studied me for a long moment before adding, "Fresh starts are needed, sometimes, to keep us sane."

She was right, of course. "What about you? I'm guessing there's a really good story behind how you ended up in this bed."

"It was just a regular skip. Nothing jumped out that told me it would go south before I introduced myself to him. He was a big bad biker daddy who skipped on a big bond. No different from any other I've taken in." She spoke with her hands, but there was pain with every move, and it reflected in the lines on her face.

"I tracked him to a bar in Fairhill." Even I knew that was the worst neighborhood in Philly, but I didn't say as much.

"I didn't even get the chance to tell him who I was before he pulled a gun and shot me." She lifted her shirt to show me a bandage, pointing to the center, which was a couple of inches above her belly button. "Bullet went in here and it tore through tissue on its way out. Missed all the important shit except a sliver of spinal tissue. Grazed it. Bruised it. Hurt it, anyway." She sighed. "Could've been way worse and I'm thanking my maker every day I'm here."

I smiled and patted her hand. "Then I will, too."

"I was in a coma for a week. Poor Tracy. That girl stayed at my bedside every single minute, praying her heart out for my recovery." She spoke with a slight southern accent, which was odd for a Philly girl and told me she wasn't from around here.

I wanted to ask her more about where she was from, but her eyelids were droopy, and her yawn full of fatigue.

Still, she continued. "I have to relearn to walk, so therapy is set up to start coming every day, starting tomorrow. I'm gonna be up chasing skips again in no time."

"I hope so." Even if it meant I was out of a job, I liked Cleo and wanted her to be at full strength. I imagined she was a whirlwind when she was at a hundred percent.

I stood because she needed her rest. "I'm going to see about breakfast and familiarize myself with your medicine. You rest, and I'll be back in a little while. Any special requests to eat?"

"Scrambled eggs would be nice." She yawned again. "But maybe in an hour or so. You are welcome to whatever is in the fridge. There's no telling what Tracy bought for food."

I helped her ease down, then left her alone and set off to take inventory of the food. As I passed her cell phone, it beeped, and a banner that said *AAA Bonds* appeared on the screen. I would've shown it to her immediately, but she needed her rest. Her injury wouldn't heal if she let herself get run down.

She awoke about an hour later, and we ate together while I asked her where she was from. She was born and raised in Tennessee and moved to Philly after she married Tracy's dad. Then after the divorce, she was down on her luck and met a bail bondsman looking for bounty hunters.

After we finished eating, I cleaned up while she settled in to watch TV. But I couldn't just sit around. I needed to be moving so I could justify charging this woman to be there. I went off in search of the laundry room to see if I could start a load for her. I passed the office first and decided to be nosy under the guise of dusting. I'd found a feather duster under the kitchen sink.

The room looked to be the same size as Cleo's bedroom. A large wooden desk that looked older than me sat in the middle of the room. Bookshelves and filing cabinets lined up against the wall that wasn't all glass. In the corner, there was a beeping fax machine with several papers gliding onto the paper tray. At first glance, the form didn't look like much more than a job application, but as it finished feeding, a picture of a woman was in the lower-left corner of the final page.

It was a bond sheet, I realized. It wasn't the same format I was used to from when I worked with my ex-husband, so I hadn't recognized it for what it was at first.

Too curious for my own good, I picked up the stack of papers. The woman had listed her occupation as an accountant—maybe Ollie knew her—and her crime was grand larceny, AKA embezzlement. The recovery fee was five grand.

Holy smokes!

Five grand to chase down a jolly-looking woman with rosy, red cheeks and a kind smile. Although I'd bet she was anything but kind.

She looked a little on the heavy side from the photo, and she was listed as only five feet and two inches tall. Just an inch taller than me.

It was too bad I couldn't go after her myself. Five grand would be a nice payday. It reminded me of when I was married to Howard. He'd brought home great money. Now I understood why Cleo had no intention to give up on her job.

With the stack of papers in my hand, I walked into Cleo's bedroom. With every word she read, her smile faded by another degree until she pushed the papers off to the side of the bed and sighed. "I wish I could take it. Sweet money for an easy skip, but it's going to be a long time before I'm up and around enough for this kind of thing."

Maybe I shouldn't have shown her the file, but on the other hand, maybe it would serve as an incentive for healing.

"Here, Hailey. Take this away. Looking at it makes me sick to my stomach." She handed me the pages. "I'm going to nap again. I swear, if I don't get out of this bed soon, I'm going to be as big as a house from all the lying around sleeping."

I walked into the living room and pulled out my smartphone. One internet search later and my cell proved its worth. The woman in the photo had "checked in" last night on BirdBook—the latest in social media trends—at the coffee shop just a few blocks from here. And according to her BirdBook page, her phone had checked her in again. Now.

Intriguing. So much so, I pictured myself

storming the building, flashing my bounty hunter ID, the crowd parting and my skip—the aforementioned plump accountant—holding her arms out in front of her for the cuffs I would slap on. I also envisioned the paycheck with my name on the *pay to the order of* line.

By the time I finished living out my fantasy, it was time to go, and I was out the door. I could totally be a bond agent. Not like 007, obviously, but I knew a thing or three about tracking down a skip from helping Howard, so I sure could track Ms. Curvy Accountant.

CHAPTER FOUR

After I parked in my driveway, I rushed straight over to Kendra's house and pounded on her door. She jerked it open with a frown, then studied me like she was waiting for me to grow a new head. "What's up with you?"

I grinned. She always knew when I was on a mission. Pushing inside, I closed the door behind us. Kendra rolled her eyes and led the way to the kitchen. "Either you have some really good dirt on someone or you're up to something."

Laughing, I handed her the fax printout of the bounty and waited while she read every line. Once, then again. "Five grand for hunting her down?"

I tapped the page with my fingertip. "I'd

forgotten how much money Howard made being a bounty hunter. I could totally do this."

Kendra eyed the page with doubt. "You're going to track down a criminal? And do what with her?"

I shrugged. "Turn her in, then collect the money." I stared back, then grinned.

"Just like that?"

"Just like that." I picked up the paper and read over the details again. "You could help. It'll be fun."

Kendra took the paper from me to read again. A slow smile formed, and I could almost see the wheels turning in her mind. "Okay. I say we do it. I'm all in."

Yes! Excitement filled me as I thought about where we'd even start to look for this woman. It was close to dinnertime so she could be home. Then again, if I had skipped out on court, I wouldn't be hanging out at my known address.

I pointed at Kendra. "You could do a locating spell."

She cocked an eyebrow. "I could."

"Then we go check it out." I wiggled my brows. "You up for the adventure?"

I loved the idea of the two of us working together. The times I'd helped Howard with his skips, I always got a thrill.

"What can it hurt? We'll see what we can find

out and maybe figure out a plan?" She had a gleam in her eyes that told me she was totally on board. Not that I was worried she wouldn't be.

Kendra was always up for a little adventure or troublemaking, depending on her mood.

Following her into the living room, I sat on the floor in front of the coffee table and instantly regretted it. I might not be able to get up now that I was down. Kendra sat on the sofa directly in front of me and smirked. "You comfy?"

"Yep, let's do this." I rubbed my hands together as I watched her pull out a map of Philly and a pendulum.

As she reached for the paper, I hesitated. "You're not going to burn it are you?"

"No." She snatched it from me and laid it on the left edge of the map, then she held the pendulum above the center of the map. She whispered a few words in a language I didn't know.

Soon the pendulum started rocking back and forth, then in a circular motion. Then it stopped over downtown. I met Kendra's gaze. "Do you have a detailed map of downtown?"

She was already slipping the map out of the hidden compartment from the coffee table. "This isn't the first time I've had to scry the city." With a wink, she quickly repeated the spell over the detailed tourist map of downtown Philly.

The pendulum stopped, and I studied the area of the map. "Is that a coffee shop?"

Kendra nodded. "They have the best pastries. Their sandwiches are amazing."

At the mention of food, my stomach growled like an angry beast, making both of us laugh. Kendra jumped up and rushed to the front door. "Are you driving, or am I?"

I rolled to my knees and grabbed a hold of the table to help push myself upright. It was uncomfortable, but I did it without help. Yay me. Maybe it was time to start working out. Or maybe walking?

Maybe I could cut back on the snacks.

Maybe not.

After Kendra stopped laughing at me and got into my car, we drove across town to the coffee shop.

Reading the file, Kendra asked, "So what does a person do to get a bounty put on them?"

Seems like something a lawyer would've known. But she mostly worked in corporate stuff. I glanced at her briefly before turning my attention to the road and where I was going. I really should have let her drive because I wasn't familiar with the roads or downtown. "Most bounties are issued by a bail bondsman because the perp skipped out on a court date or a check in after being bonded out of jail."

Kendra glanced up and pointed. "Turn at the next right. Then find a place to park."

Nodding, I switched on the blinker. "Sometimes bounty hunters will get private jobs to track down someone. But this bounty came from a bondsman, so I'm not worried about dealing with shady people."

"Shady as in paranormal, or shady as in mafia?" I could just see her skeptical look from the corner of my eye.

I snorted. "Maybe both."

Sucking in a breath, she nodded. "You're right."

I pulled into a spot about a half-block from our destination and smiled. "Parking gods are smiling on us. It's a sign."

"It's a parking spot." Kendra's flat voice made me chuckle. For being a witch, she always had one foot stuck firmly in the cement of reality. "I think a sign would be like running into the woman we're looking for, and her surrendering peacefully. That would mean this is what we're meant to do with our lives."

I chuffed at her. "Where did the 'go get 'em girl enthusiasm' go? The what-can-it-hurt logic that's ninety-four percent of the reason we were on the case in the first place?"

"Ninety-four percent?" She arched an eyebrow. "That's awfully specific."

"Mama needs the money is the other six percent." I shrugged, and she laughed as we crossed at the light.

Kendra snorted. "Funny, I thought it was the other way around."

She wasn't wrong there, but I was excited about this case.

Instead of staying at the Cup o' the Morning Coffee House after we took a quick look around for our skip, who wasn't there, we decided to have lunch at a sidewalk cafe across the street and watch for her. They had chilled wine breezers as well as the best cheese and charcuterie trays in the state of Pennsylvania. And when the tray was gone, we moved onto loaded nachos, then bruschetta and pita chips. By the time we decided to give up and go home, I was in carb overload. I'd probably have to lay off them for the next week or two. I didn't have the metabolism of a twenty-year-old anymore.

"I don't think she's going to show." I sat back in the black iron chair and pushed my hair behind my ear. "I don't understand it. She was here, right? How accurate is the locator spell?"

She too sat back; her lips twisted. "Accurate

enough, but that doesn't mean she couldn't have left while we drove over here."

Yeah, that made sense. Darn it.

Unfortunately for us, it meant a cold trail just when I'd been excited about being on the case. On the hunt. Doing something for once in my life. I sighed. "Well, let's go home and come up with a plan B."

Kendra nodded. We'd paid as we went along, so we didn't have to wait for a bill before we left. I stood and pushed my chair in, then looked at the number of plates left on the table. "Good thing she didn't show up. If she ran, no way was I catching her." I slid my arm through Kendra's. "Roll me to the car."

She chuckled, then stopped. Stared. Or maybe gaped was a better word. Open-mouthed gawking. No matter what I called it, she saw something and stopped, giving me time so I would see it too. I followed her gaze. "Well, I'll be damned. Would ya look at that?"

In front of us, walking as if she didn't have a care in the world, was Zara—the skip. She was wearing a black hoodie with the hood on, but no doubt, it was her. The reason she used the Cup O' the Morning Coffee House was because it was close to her house.

She made a left into a parking garage.

I glanced at the building and the street sign on the corner. "That's her building. Why on Earth would she use the address the bondsman had?"

"Maybe she's arrogant enough to think she wouldn't get caught."

Zara would have to be. Either that or stupid. I was going with a little of both.

We followed close, but not so close she would hear the tap of our shoes against the concrete. We stopped when Zara did and flattened ourselves against the wall as Zara took the stairs. We hopped into the conveniently empty and waiting elevator and went up a level.

When the doors whooshed open, Zara was at the far end of the garage, walking through another door. This time, we followed, racing through the open air to where she'd disappeared. But before I could reach for the knob, an arm stretched out and clotheslined me. I was flung backward and landed on my ass. My throat closed up where the arm hit me, and I had to fight just to suck in just a little bit of air.

Kendra had her hands about four inches apart in front of her, summoning the energy she would need for the binding spell. She spoke the words in Latin, because it always had to be Latin instead of just *so-*

*and-so, I bind you to so-and-so!* Or whatever the words meant.

While she weaved her spell, I took a slight pummeling as I tried to breathe. If I could get my breath, I could fight back at least a little, but being clotheslined had really taken me down.

I just had to wait for the words to work their magic but tucking and rolling wasn't doing me any good. "Ken?" I gasped as I rolled away from Zara's kick. "You got anything?"

She might've said run. Or none. Or done. I couldn't tell because all I saw was a giant hand—it was probably normal sized, but I was a teeny bit overwhelmed—reaching for me and pulling me into the darkness. Someone, or something, had yanked me into an alcove, a very very dark alcove.

But then a sliver of light from the outer garage shone on what could only have been fangs one second before they plunged into my throat.

Then the world went black.

## CHAPTER FIVE

My head was being held in a vice. The vice tightened every second. The pressure pounded in my temples, which was getting worse with all the noise. Every sound was amplified to ear-splitting decibels, and I ached like I'd been hit by a train, then knocked under a falling tree.

Then the tree caught on fire before being doused with acid.

In other words, ouch.

As soon as I peeled my eyes open, I first realized I was home; then I noticed I was in my room, and it was night. Those were the things I knew for sure. The rest... I had nothing. No idea how I got home from the parking garage. No idea why my head hurt or why my house was so loud.

A flash of a memory went off in my mind. Fangs. I'd been bitten by something with fangs. What the hell was that about? It was the last thing I remembered.

Kendra's voice was loud, so damned loud. It was like I could hear her hair moving. Really? That wasn't even possible. Whatever the noise was, it couldn't have been her hair.

Then again, my bestie was a witch with real magical abilities. That wasn't supposed to be real either. Yet here we were.

I opened my mouth to let her know I was awake, and to ask her to quiet down, but I couldn't speak. My throat was too dry and scratchy. The only sound that came out was a deep sounding squeak. Like a cow being choked to death.

Sexy.

I turned my head to look at the table where a glass of beautiful crystal-clear water sat waiting on me. Oh, thank God. I only needed a sip, to wet my whistle.

I sat up, grabbed the glass, and tipped it to my lips. Cool refreshment washed down my throat and the sandpaper eased enough so I could shout.

"Hey!"

But as soon as I spat the word, I choked the water

back up and out. It dribbled it down the front of my nightgown. I must've drunk it too fast.

The door flung open revealing Kendra and Jaxon —my hot neighbor from across the street. They stopped just inside the door frame, in silhouette thanks to the hall light behind them, but there was no mistaking either one. Plus, I was new in Philly. I didn't know anyone beside these two, Cleo and her daughter. Of course, my brothers. And whatever the hell bit me.

"Why are you here?" I croaked. It was all I could think clearly enough to ask. Now, I was parched again. So damned thirsty. I reached for the glass again.

"Are you feeling okay?" Kendra sat beside me on the bed.

Jax moved around to sit on the other side. "You've been asleep for a while."

After staring at Jax for a second too long, wondering again why he was in my bedroom, I looked from one of them to the other. They looked concerned. I still needed a drink. No way was I going to be able to talk until I got a damned drink.

Kendra laid her hand on my forehead then glanced at Jax. They shared a look. "What?" I tried, but nothing came out. Again.

"Oh, tell me you remember," she gasped. "Holy shiznet, Hails. We were at the garage, do you remember?" She didn't wait for me to answer. "This woman, the skip? She attacked. Had you on the ground and my spell didn't work!" Her voice tore through my skull, but I remembered. The images of what had happened flashed through my mind. Not that it mattered, because as Kendra spoke, she waved her arms. A lot.

The one closest to me... Oh, my. It looked like the juiciest, most flavorful turkey leg I'd ever seen before in forty years of Thanksgiving dinners. I ignored the ringing in my head, the pain from her volume, everything that wasn't her delectable, mouth-watering arm.

I followed it with my eyes, with my head, until I had the moves down, and I knew what she was going to do. I reached out for a bite. Just one. It was all I needed. A nibble.

She jerked back, and I recoiled in horror, wanting to smack myself. I should've grabbed it with my hands first. Duh.

"What the hell are you doing?" Her appalled face wasn't as intense as my hunger, and my tongue swiped across my lips.

Jax held up one hand. "It's normal, Kendra. She's fine."

"What's normal?" I whispered. My throat felt like dust. When the heck did we normalize that? Lusting for a taste of my best friend's arm? Wait. Why did I want to eat Kendra's arm?

A second after I had the thought, I didn't care. I wanted a bite. She was back to talking. "...she bit you and we had to act fast." Her arm moved left. I faded with it. "Stop looking at me like I'm lunch." She hugged it closer to herself, but then the other arm looked just as good. "Jax?"

"Right." He sighed. "She isn't going to be worth much until she eats."

"Yeah. I'm starving." I didn't know if the words made it past my parched throat or if I imagined them, but the sentiment stood. I liked the way he thought. Food.

Before I could try to speak again, Luke burst into my room and pushed between them like a bright, delicious-smelling roast beef sandwich. The closer he came, the louder his heartbeat sounded, and the better he smelled.

Wait! Why was I imagining my brother as food? Better yet, why was I so damn hungry? What had bitten me?

My mind was too muddled to put it all together, even though all the clues pointed toward only one possibility.

Luke plopped down on the bed. "I have been trying to call you for days. Your voicemail box is full, FYI." He gave a sideways head bob, then I grabbed him without a second thought, pulled him close, and sank my teeth into his soft, warm flesh. Blood spilled between my lips. Effervescent. Delicious.

Better than any gourmet meal I'd ever eaten, more satisfying than the greasiest burger or the savoriest soup. This was Nirvana. Heavenly. My own garden of Eden.

Then he jerked back—more accurately, Jax pulled him back. Luke slapped his hand over his artery. "You bit me?" He glared at me with wide eyes. "*Bit me?!*"

I shrugged. He had roughly a gallon and a half of blood in his body. No way had I taken enough to matter.

Then, I froze. As a cloud of confusion lifted from my hazy, food deprived brain, reality slammed into me. I'd bitten him. Drank his *blood*.

Horrified, I jumped up from the bed and rushed into the bathroom. After slamming the door shut, I stared at myself in the mirror. Besides the bedhead, I looked *great*. Fantastic, really. My once imperfect skin was flawless, even though it looked pale.

Then I opened my mouth, and my suspicions were confirmed.

I had fangs.

I poked at them with my index finger, wondering if they went away and only appeared when I was hungry. I frowned, turning to sag against the counter. So many questions swarmed my brain. Jax would have the answers.

I jumped out of my skin when someone pounded on the bathroom door. Then Luke screeched through the wood. "Hailey Marie Louise Whitfield!"

I giggled and opened the door. "Uh-oh. It's a full name assault." Then I stared at Luke, who stared back at me with wide-eyes and his mouth hanging open. I darted a glance to Kendra then back at my brother. "What?"

"You bit me! You freaking bit me!" He touched his neck with his fingers and showed them to me. "You drew blood."

I stared at the tips of his fingers coated in crimson. I swiped my tongue out, catching a small drop of leftover blood from the corner of my mouth. A second wave of Utopian happiness washed over me.

Lightning quick, I wrapped my fingers around his wrist. "Come here."

He jerked his hand away from me and held it to his chest, his features a mask of horror. "Stay away from me," he whispered.

A pang of sadness washed over me. I knew my actions weren't normal, but I couldn't help it. Luke had tasted so yummy. Okay, no. That was my brother. He was not food.

Brothers were friends. Not food.

I drifted closer to Jax. Surely, being a vampire himself, he'd stop me if I went crazy. At least, I hoped he would.

Luke was still being dramatic about the whole thing. He turned on Kendra and put his hands on his hips. "What the hell is wrong with Hailey? I want answers, and I want them now because I am *freaking* out. And bleeding."

"Breathe, Luke. Just breathe." Kendra led him away while Jax took my hand and pulled me toward the bed to sit down with him.

It took a second, but my mind cleared. Somewhat. Although I could still smell Kendra and Luke, I got nothing from Jax. Well, nothing but the desire to lick every inch of him and that had nothing to do with eating...erm drinking. "Why can't I smell you?"

"Because you're a freaking vampire." Kendra shrieked the words at me, waving her hands.

"A *what* now?" Luke turned to her as she sat him down and handed him a cloth to put over his bite. "I'm gonna need a bigger story here."

Kendra nodded. "Yeah." She told him everything, and bits of memory came back to me with each word until I had a whole picture.

Zara had turned me.

"She's a vampire? You'd think they'd put something like that on the bond sheet." I huffed out a breath. Then again, humans wouldn't know what Zara was because vamps and other paranormal creatures did whatever they could to live in secret, just like Kendra did.

"After you passed out, she took off. I screamed for help, and Jax showed up." She nodded to him.

"I'd been tracking Zara, too. I almost had her, but then..." He shrugged, and it didn't take a genius to know he thought we'd gotten in the way. "I got a call for help. I smelled the blood, saw the teeth marks, and I knew what she'd done."

"Holy crap." The situation probably warranted something a little stronger—something that started with an F at least—but I was all kinds of hopped up on Luke blood. And Lukey blood was *good* blood.

Jax waved his hand. "Yeah. Killing humans is a big no-no in the vamp world. So is turning them, for that matter. There's a council that governs the whole race. I didn't have any choice but to turn you." His apology was so heartfelt, it said this euphoria wasn't going to last and things were going to go south eventually. No one would apologize for this kind of rapture, the ecstasy, the bliss.

"So, we took you home and you've been asleep for the last three days." Kendra finished the story, but I stopped listening after *three days*.

"I have to go to work. Oh, God. I can't afford to lose that job, I just got it and I really like her!" I said every word in a single breath, which considering I was a vampire, I probably didn't even have to breathe anymore. Did I? I tried to hold my breath, but I was too upset.

Kendra moved closer until I couldn't help it any longer and licked my lips again. Then she took a step back. "I called and told her you'd been in a car accident."

Luke swiveled from looking at me to glaring at her. "You remembered the boss she worked for *one day with*, but not her beloved older brother?" he snarled out in a breath.

Kendra brushed him off. "I would've called, but I've been busy worrying about my best friend."

"Watching her sleep?" His volume climbed. "How busy could you be?"

Kendra puffed up her chest. "Listen, bucko, I sat at her bedside. Held her hand. Chanted a mantra so good—"

"A mantra? You chanted *a mantra?*" He mimicked her lighter tone, cocked his hip on the chair, then held up a finger. "Let me tell you something, *best friend.* I am the first call. Always."

They argued back and forth. She reminded him I was in my forties and didn't need my brother. He said I was younger than him and would be until one of us died. I wanted to jump in with a walking dead joke, but Jax shook his head when I opened my mouth.

It was like he could read my thoughts. That was something I wasn't ready to know about at the moment.

"Some things are better left alone." He nodded to Kendra and Luke, still bickering. "That's one of them." Then he stood and ushered them out of the room, shut the door behind them, locked it, and crossed back to the empty side of my bed. He pulled back the blanket and slid in.

"Uh…" I scooted over to give him room on the bed. It was a good thing I had a king size. At least I didn't run the risk of biting *him*. "What are you doing?"

"Your body is still adjusting to the changes, and you should rest. But I have some things to explain, first." He gave me a soft, sweet, dreamy look. "You're going to need to feed often right now. And until you learn to control your impulses, I need to stay with you."

Stay with me? Yeah. Good plan, right there. How the hell was I going to focus with mister hottie vampire in my house. All. The. Time. "Okay." Maybe we could snuggle, too.

"There are rules, Hailey. Not many, but they are in place to keep the race from being detected by humans. One of those rules is we are not allowed to turn humans without the council's permission." He paused, as if giving me time to absorb what he'd said.

"I take it you didn't have permission to turn me?"

He nodded. "I did not."

My gut twisted with worry. "Then why did you?" He didn't know me, so why risk punishment?

Jaxon rolled to his side and stared at me for a long while. "I have my reasons, so don't worry about the council. I'll deal with them."

I'd do as he asked and let him worry about that. "You said there are other rules?"

"Besides keeping the existence of vampires a secret, the others are more like guidelines. I am the master vampire for the Philadelphia and surrounding areas. I set the rules for my territory. My biggest rule is to not bite unwilling humans. I own a club that is strictly for paranormal beings only. I have humans that work for me that vampires can feed on." I must have made a face because he paused and laughed. "It's not that bad. The humans are loyal and have full knowledge of us."

I thought about it for a few moments. That was a handy way to deal with the feeding issue. It was a relief that I wouldn't be going around biting random people. "What happens if one of the humans betrays your trust in them?"

"Their memories are erased, and they are encouraged to move out of town so there is no risk of their memories coming back." His tone was so matter of fact, but there was a note of something else in his words.

I narrowed my gaze. "If their memories return?"

He sighed and brushed a stray strand of hair from my cheek, leaving chill bumps in his wake.

Good to know I could still get chill bumps. "I don't kill them unless I have no other choice."

I nodded and stared at the ceiling, then yawned. So, he would kill a human when necessary. Would I?

Jax gave my hand a squeeze. "As your sire, it is my job to train you. But for now, you need to rest."

I smiled; not sure I could sleep anymore. After all, I had slept for three days! "Will you stay?" When he nodded, I blew out another breath.

He settled in against the pillow, and I turned to look at him. The full-on view was breathtaking. Wasn't every day I had a gorgeous vampire in my bed. Or anyone gorgeous, vampire or not.

I watched him for a few seconds. "Does this mean I can never go to the beach again?" Not that I was much of a sun worshipper, but I loved the sand and the ocean, and the smell of it all.

"You can, but you'll only get a few good minutes before you burst into flames, and maybe one more minute before you're a pile of ash. Or you could go at night." He could've just said no. But he had to go for the dramatic.

"And garlic?" I loved walking by Juliano's Eatery. They had the most aromatic dishes on their menu.

"Myth. Doesn't hurt us. Crosses are also a myth of epic proportion." He reached over to brush my bangs off my forehead, and if I still had circulation, my blood would've rushed to my heart. "You can see your reflection in a mirror."

So, the latter, I found out when I rushed to the bathroom after biting Luke. "Good. Bad hair days are okay every once in a while, but...a girl needs to see herself." I frowned. This was a lot to digest. "At least, I get the super speed, right?" Maybe I would finally run that marathon I'd always dreamed of.

"Maybe. Our kind isn't a class you can fit in a box. Some of us are strong, some can see in the dark, some are fast, others hear really well. A few of us are blessed enough to have all the..." He grinned. "Superpowers."

"How'd you get so lucky?" I wasn't jealous. More like intrigued. More so than I'd ever been.

He winked. "I'm going to help you get through this."

"As my maker?" And lover?

He smiled again. "And a friend." Ah, well.

I wanted to thank him, to be grateful, but I was a vampire who would never feel the sun on my face again. I was tired and hungry. For blood. There was a lot to unpack before I would be able to work my way around to gratitude for his saving my life.

"How old are you?" I asked. It didn't matter, really, but I was curious.

Jaxon sucked in a breath. "More than a century."

Oh geez. Talk about a May-December relationship. "I have a lot more stuff to learn, huh?"

"There's time." But even at a hundred plus years old, he wasn't a good enough liar to sneak a deception past a woman who'd already been lied to by a husband and a half. Of course, right now, I wasn't worried about the lies. I was worried that I had a gorgeous man beside me. In my bed.

And all I wanted was to drink my brother's blood.

# CHAPTER SIX

I woke up again on Sunday, after sunset. I hadn't really given much thought to whether or not vampires slept, but it seemed to me maybe I didn't think they did. Then again, Jax had encouraged me to rest so maybe they did? But here I was, four days into a long and somewhat broken nap, and I was a vampire.

Thank God I didn't have to sleep in a coffin.

I hoped this fatigue didn't last and was just part of the transformation process. That was another thing I'd add to my growing list of questions for Jax. Right now, I needed to get my ducks in a row because, vampire or not, I still had to pay for a place to live and that meant I had to work.

I picked up my phone from the table and dialed Cleo.

She answered on the third ring. "Hello?"

She sounded strong, and not angry despite caller ID, so I hoped it was a good sign. "Hi, Cleo. It's Hailey."

"How are you doing?" The concern was comforting.

"I'm fine. I just wanted to apologize and let you know I'm going to have to adjust my shifts." Shame and guilt bubbled inside me for lying. Well, technically I didn't lie. Kendra had. For me.

"All right. I can work with that. I had to hire someone for the day shifts anyway, but we're still looking for a part time night shift person." The sound of papers rustling filtered through the line.

Relief flooded me that I hadn't lost my job. That was perfect. Luck was finally smiling on me. "Thank you." There was no way I could make it without the income from that job. I could maybe go part time now that I wouldn't have to buy food. "Thank you so much."

"Tracy has it covered for the next two nights, so how about you start back on Tuesday night?"

The next time I saw her, I was going to give her

the biggest, strongest hug I could manage without injuring her.

When I hung up, Jax was standing in the doorway to my bedroom, hands in his pockets, shoulders braced against the door frame. Damn, he looked good. "Good morning."

Morning was about twelve hours ago, but in this circumstance, it made sense. "Hi."

His slow smile sent warmth burning along my nerve endings, and I would've thought I had blood flowing through my veins, but I knew otherwise. Still, the effect was the same.

He looked me up and down, then shook his head and smiled. "You slept for three or four days, and you look amazing."

"Maybe that's my vampire superpower." Not the most functional of gifts, but I could make it work.

He chuckled. "Come on. You need to eat."

At first, I thought he was inviting me to my own kitchen, but then I remembered. A wave of sadness hit as it occurred to me that I would never again eat in my own kitchen. Not food anyway. I wondered if I would miss the taste of comforting favorites like cheese and fried chicken.

Immortality was a trade-off for taste buds, and I wasn't sure I was down with it. I really liked to eat.

I stepped into the bathroom to get ready, but... my hair was full and lustrous, and my skin shined like a toddler's who'd never been kissed by the sun. Just for good measure, I brushed my teeth carefully. My fangs were still out and sensitive! After a change into less wrinkly clothes—I still hadn't unpacked them all—we headed downstairs.

When we were in the car, Jax glanced over at me. "You okay?"

I wasn't. This was a lot to take in. Maybe the sleep was my subconscious trying to hide from the reality of my new lifestyle. But telling him wasn't very otherworldly of me, so I didn't answer. Instead, I asked my own question. Avoidance was a good friend to have at that moment. "Where are we going?"

"The club I own downtown." He started the car, and within moments we were on the road.

I remembered him saying he owned a club for the paranormal during one of the times I'd woken. "Does this club have a name?"

"It's called 'Catch and Release.'"

"Catchy. Decorated in a fishing motif?" Made sense in my head.

"No." His focus was wholly on the road, as if he didn't drive much and this made him nervous.

Maybe he didn't. I would ask another time. "It's more about the patrons. I opened the club with the idea to help vampires feed without risking discovery. It was more popular than I'd imagined. Eventually other paranormals started to come. It's one of the few safe places they have to be who they are without hiding."

"That is where dinner is tonight." I was okay with that. The thought of lurking in the shadows and waiting on an unsuspecting human to feed on made me want to cry. There was comfort in knowing that the person I feed from tonight would be all knowing.

"How often will I need to feed?" I asked.

Jax glanced at me, then quickly focused back on the road. "Right now, once a day or every other day. Once you're a little older and more controlled, you won't have to feed as often. Maybe once or twice a week."

How much older were we talking? Because that sounded much better than dealing with this insatiable hunger. "Like years?"

"No." Oh, thank God. "It varies. Could be a couple of months." I could live with that. "Could be a bit longer. In rare cases, a couple of weeks."

Again, too vague for comfort. "Is there anything else I need to know?"

He nodded. I knew there would be. "If you lose too much blood or wait too long to eat, you'll go through a period where you need to eat more in a shorter period of time." I wasn't up on vampire lore. The things I knew about witches came from Kendra, but we hadn't talked much about vamps until I'd moved next door to one and then the extent of our conversations had been that my neighbors were vampires. "Feeding isn't sensual or sexual," he continued. "Though some of the romance novels make me wish it was."

I chuckled. I'd read those books, too. I could buy that as far as when *I* was feeding. But I couldn't imagine Jax doing anything and it not looking sensual and sexual. Sinful. The thought of his mouth anywhere near a pulse point of mine would've done exciting and crazy things to me... if I still had a pulse.

"Okay," I squeaked.

He smiled and gave my hand a squeeze where it laid on my lap. There was something to be said for this man's touch. He used it in all the best ways. "I only feed about once a week. It doesn't take nearly as much to satisfy me."

I totally didn't focus on the way he said, *satisfy me*. Because I was a grown woman who knew how to control herself. I hadn't jumped his bones yet, had I?

Instead, I focused on the benefit of his words.

"Imagine how much extra time you have without having to worry about cooking or eating."

I smiled, and without thinking said, "I would finally have time to plant a garden." Then it dawned on me. "Except I would have to do it by twilight." Ugh.

"I've always been partial to night blooming jasmine." Another squeeze of my hand before he let go and resumed his grip of the steering wheel. "Moon flowers are pretty too."

Night blooming jasmine. Maybe I could plant that garden, then. I'd do my best to look on the bright side.

We pulled into the parking lot, and he walked around to help me out of the car. I didn't really need the help or expect it, and it was so very old-fashioned, but I smiled. He seemed to be the kind of guy I'd thought Brad had been. Boy had I been wrong.

I walked beside him inside the club. I'd expected low, eardrum bursting music, but it wasn't loud at all. Instead, the club was filled with upbeat, electro-dance-type music, but not overly loud, maybe because vampires had sensitive hearing. For that I was glad. I was getting too old for a lot of noise. My ears wanted to crawl away from all the noises. The car had helped, blocking out some of the outside sounds, and surprisingly, this music helped quite a bit. Maybe I'd invest in some really good earbuds when I got a paycheck.

"The club is two-story," Jax said as we made our way to a set of spiral stairs to the right of the main entrance.

I slowed and scanned the lower level. The club had an old gothic-style look. The color scheme of the club was red and black with gold accents. *Better to hide the blood.*

There were tall, round tables with fancy bar stools at each one scattered around the dance floor in the center of the room. Booths and other casual living room-style seating filled up the space along the walls. There were two bars, one at each end of the ground floor.

Glancing back at Jax, I realized he was halfway up the stairs, so I rushed forward to follow him up.

The second level had less seating available than the first. It seemed much more private too. Groups of high-back sofas that curved in half circles about the size of a loveseat framed by matching armchairs were randomly placed around the floor.

The upper floor also had two bars, as well as an area with pool tables and dart boards.

Jaxon walked beside me, his hand at the small of my back and, whether I imagined it or not, he filled me with warmth. There was something about this guy and the way my body reacted to him. I just couldn't pinpoint why or how.

He guided me to a section above the dancefloor with plush seating and mirrored walls. Swiping out an arm to the vampires sitting in that cozy seating area. "Hailey, this is my clan." They stood, and a man took one step forward. "Ransom, my brother and my right hand," Jaxon said.

Ransom held out his hand, and I shook it, but couldn't stop marveling at how much they looked alike and how pleasing those looks were. The resemblance was striking as far as chiseled features and pale, creamy skin. But where Jax had strawberry blond hair and blue eyes, his brother had hair the color of milk chocolate and the eyes to match.

"This is Paige." Jax indicated the woman next to Ransom.

I nodded and smiled. I'd seen some beautiful women before, but this one had cheekbones and lashes to die for. Her coal black hair was sleek and off her face. Her rich, brown skin glowed under the strobing lights of the club.

"Grim." Jax continued, nodding toward another man.

Grim stood and thrust out his hand. Smiling. I shook his hand and he nodded at Jax, then moved back to his chair. He was rougher looking; big, built like half a building with tawny beige skin and eyes as dark as a midnight sky.

"And finally, this is Nash."

Nash nodded and slung his arm across the back of Paige's seat. There wasn't much about Nash to comment on except to say he reminded me of a chameleon; his long face gave the impression he would fit in anywhere.

Maybe that was his vampire power. Blending in.

"Nash and Grim report to Paige, but they're all enforcers."

I wasn't sure what an enforcer did, but I liked that a woman was in control.

Jax led me around, helped me pick some humans for feeding then showed me how to make it happen. It wasn't much different than when I bit Luke except the humans in the bar knew what to expect.

He also showed me that to cover the bite marks, I only needed to lick over the bite and my saliva sealed up the holes like magic. Neat-o.

Jaxon included memory-altering in his brief

training session. Which I would need to learn in case I had to feed and couldn't make it to the club. That was a skill I learned quickly.

When I finished feeding, I smiled at Jax. He really was gorgeous. I felt twenty years younger, stronger, and more alive for someone whose heart wasn't even beating anymore. Dear God, Jax was beautiful. Did I mention that already? I danced over to him and slid my arms around his neck.

I never did this kind of thing. Never had this kind of fun. It was exhilarating.

Jaxon cleared his throat and gently pulled my arms down. "I should get you home. Start training you."

Duty always got in the way of a good time. It didn't look like being a vampire was going to change that.

I nodded but frowned. I couldn't help it. I wanted a moment. A memory. I didn't know whether or not being changed was something to celebrate. Not for more than it had kept me alive, but I was having fun. I hadn't let loose like this in decades.

"Should we say goodbye to the clan?" I asked.

He nodded. "Sure."

Maybe I knew they would insist we stay. Or maybe I just hoped they would, and to my delight they did. "Nah, come on, Jax. Stay. Have fun," Nash said.

Paige chimed in with Nash's argument. "She's new. Let her celebrate. Find her place."

Ransom stood and put his hands on his brother's shoulders. "And what's the point in having a bar if you don't indulge every once in a while?"

Paige crossed her arms and cocked her head. "Did you tell her?" Her grin spread across her face as she leaned in. "Do you feel it? The blood from a drunk human is such a buzz. It's the beauty of Jax owning this place." She put her arm around me. "Look at them."

Bodies writhed to the deep, loud bass line of whatever music this was. Couples dancing close. Others gyrating into the air. But everyone had a drink, and everyone was smiling. This was the life I'd missed by marrying young and not finding out who I was first. I hadn't experienced anything like this before.

I glanced at Jax, who was busy staring at me. He asked, "You want to stay?"

I did. More than anything. I nodded.

With a shrug, he sighed and chuckled. "All right. We'll stay."

And before I could rethink it, I threw my arms

around his neck and pulled him down so I could press a hard kiss against his mouth. Then, I let him go like it was the kind of thing I did all the time.

It wasn't. But the look he gave me when I pulled back made it all worth it.

## CHAPTER SEVEN

According to Jax, for the time being, I was going to have to feed at least once a night, although the amount I would need at each feeding wasn't too much. True to his word, when I awoke Monday night, I was hungry. Again. Apparently, it was the hunger I had to learn to control, but to start the small feedings would help. Kind of like a new diet. I'd been on enough of those to understand the notion.

At least I could use the club for feeding. Plus, it was fun.

As far as useful information, it was like DIY for new vamps, and I couldn't believe he'd left me on my own already. What if I failed?

No, I would not think like that. *I will not fail!*

I called Kendra and Luke, and when they came over, I gave them each a bracelet Jax had helped me make to repel vamps. That was when I found out that he knew a witch who had made the anti-compulsion charms. That had sparked a bunch of questions that Jax didn't have time for. At least at the moment. He'd had some kind of meeting to go to. But he promised we'd have time to chat soon.

I was looking forward to spending time alone with him.

The main reason I reached out to Kendra and Luke was because who else was I going to ask to go with me to a vampire bar? Not just a bar owned by a vampire. A bar where vampires foraged humans for their sustenance. And what if every vamp didn't have someone like Jax to see them through the changing, the feeding? The thought made me glad for the bracelets. I didn't even know if vampires bit other vamps, but I also didn't want to take the chance.

Jax had said that vampires couldn't compel their own kind, our own kind, but sometimes a really old vamp could influence a newbie easily enough. That was enough motivation to get a bracelet for myself.

When we got to the club, the music pulsed and

the bodies gyrated, but I was in a get in and get right back out kind of mood.

Kendra stopped and stared as Ransom approached. My new senses helped me understand Luke was about to burst from nervousness. He was like a shaking chihuahua, though he contained it. I probably wouldn't have noticed when I was human.

"Hello, Hailey." He gave each of us a quick once-over and his eyes lingered for an extra second on Luke. "Who're your friends?"

After I introduced them, we stood in an awkward little circle until Luke smiled. He'd over-come his nerves, apparently. "Hey, Halo, do they have anything here to drink that doesn't have an RH factor?" Luke nudged me, and boytoy he was, smiled at Ransom.

I glanced at Ransom, who wasn't built to be a boytoy, but he watched until Luke quit gyrating to the beat of the music. "We have a fully stocked bar of top shelf liquor."

Kendra slipped one arm through mine and waved her free hand toward the dance floor. "See anything that looks like a T-bone? A Big Mac maybe?"

I snorted at her attempt at a joke. She was trying to be funny, and I appreciated her attempt at lightening the mood, but this was serious business. Jax had been clear. The hunger could drive me mad and cause me to lose control. Since Kendra had gone with the food reference, I wasn't seeing a bunch of twenty-something humans getting their groove on, I was seeing dancing steak and burgers.

"It's not like heading to the grocery store and picking out a cut of meat, Ken." I rolled my eyes, then leaned in close to her. "You of all people should know that vampires have amazing hearing.

Luke reappeared without Ransom, but with a frozen margarita for Kendra and a martini garnished with a green apple slice. "Sure, it is," he said. "What are you in the mood for?"

Apparently, my brother had picked up on our conversation.

Just then, a well-built male human with a polo and khakis tight enough I could see his religion walked past, and Luke followed with his eyes and the turn of his head toward me. "He looks tasty. Banana cream pie tasty."

I laughed a little as he sipped and stared over the rim of his glass. I didn't care who I fed on, but the thirst was powerful.

Instead of standing and gawking, I pulled Kendra onto the dancefloor while Luke perused the clientele, then when something of the tall, dark, and dumb as a brick variety grinded into the group, I quirked my finger at him and motioned for him to follow me to a dark corner. If he didn't know what I wanted, it didn't matter. In ten minutes, he wouldn't remember me anyway. And all the humans in here had been pre-warned. That was the deal and why it had taken us a moment to get in. The bouncer had cleared Luke and Kendra. I wrapped my arms around his neck and bit, only drinking enough to slake my thirst, then closed up the holes and wiped his memory. "That was a nice hug," I said as I stared deeply into his eyes. "Thank you."

He walked away with a dumb, but happy smile on his face, though I was still hungry.

There was a safe way out of this. I could just ask one of the vampire servers there to bring me some-one. Jax hired humans that were loyal to him and his clan and worked here to feed Jax's VIPs. Since I was now considered one of Jax's vamps, that included me. But I needed to learn to feed, erase, and let go. AKA Catch and Release.

Hence the name of the bar. So clever.

I scanned the dance floor while Kendra and I moved to the beat until a cute, young man caught my attention. I offered him a closed lip smile. That was invitation enough for him because he moved through the sea of bodies straight for me.

"Hi, I'm Grey. Would you like to dance? Maybe a bite as well?" He winked and smiled at me, showing the cutest dimples.

"Sure." I offered my hand to him. "Lead the way."

Grey took my hand and pulled me out to the center of the dance floor. Just as we stopped the music switched to a slow song. Perfect! I wasn't sure why I felt the need to conceal my feeding. That was the point of the club, after all.

Gripping my hips, Grey pulled me close and began to sway. I enjoyed the dance for a little while before I couldn't fight off the hunger anymore. Not because it was trying to take over, but because I didn't want to lose control when Jax wasn't around. I needed to prove I could do this on my own—without the fanged babysitter. Ransom was here for that reason; I knew that the moment I saw him. But lucky for me, Luke was currently distracting him at the bar.

I fed from Grey and danced some more, then fed again quickly before I closed the holes and stepped away from him. As I turned to walk away, he grabbed my arm tight enough that his fingers dug into my muscle.

My gaze locked with his, and I asked, "What is your problem?"

"Don't you want to feed some more?" He loosened his hold and slid his hand down my arm to my waist. Desire flared in his eyes, and I frowned.

Grey wanted more than just to feed me his blood. Well, he was about to get his bubble burst. I flatted a hand to his chest and gave a gentle push. "I'm done."

He pouted and covered my hand with his. "Oh, come on. Just one more taste. I know you like it. I sure did." To prove his point, he took my hand and placed it on the crotch of his jeans. By the feel of it, the package behind the denim was impressive.

Too bad. I wasn't in the mood to be seduced by Grey, the blood junkie. I grabbed a hold of his bulge and squeezed, bringing a whimper from him. Then I spoke through my teeth while making eye contact. "When a lady—human or vampire—says she is done or says no in any form, she means it. Don't come on to her like a crackhead needing his next fix. You hear me?"

He nodded while swallowing hard. A slight tremble went through his body, so I released his erection before causing permanent damage. "Forget we ever met and go home to sleep it off."

With a slight nod, he walked off. That was when Kendra made an appearance. She touched my arm, making me jump. "Sorry. I didn't mean to startle you. Are you okay?"

"Yeah." I watched Grey disappear out the front door, then met Kendra's concerned stare. "I'm fine."

Then I led Kendra to the bar where Luke was chatting with Ransom. Tugging on Luke's arm sleeve, I said, "Come on. Let's go."

Ransom caught my gaze. "You did the right thing out there."

I wanted to ask him if that was normal, but I didn't want to talk about it right then. Jax was coming over for training later, so I'd ask him. "I know." I didn't need a man telling me how to handle men. I'd done it for forty years. Ransom meant well, but ugh.

Luke, who didn't seem to hear Ransom's and my exchange of words, grinned at me. "You go ahead. I'll be along later." His brow wiggle accompanied a lean-in for a hug.

After hugging him, I asked, "Are you sure?"

Ransom slid a hand over the back of Luke's chair. "I'll take good care of your brother, Hails."

Oh, I bet he would. I hesitated for a long few moments. "Okay. Call me when you get home. If I don't answer, I died a final death during training with Jax."

Luke waved me off like I was interrupting private time with his new vampy crush. Laughing, I gave him a kiss on the cheek, then Kendra and I were off.

IT WAS JUST AFTER MIDNIGHT, and I was standing in front of my closet. I wasn't sure what to wear anymore. Pajamas were my daytime attire now, but it felt odd to change out of my club outfit and not into PJs.

After a little longer, I settled on a pair of exercise pants and a Bon Jovi t-shirt. Not long after I changed, Jax knocked on my door. "Come on. Time to train."

I wasn't sure I liked the way he said train. He'd mentioned honing my skills, harnessing my strength, and finding my vampire power, if I had any special ability. But now he made it sound like we were going to get sweaty and not in a fun way.

I walked beside him to his house across the street, more specifically around his house and through the gate in the obscenely tall fence around the back yard. And by *obscenely tall,* I meant definitely higher than the eight-foot zoning restriction fence. But the fence wasn't the reason for my open-mouth gaping. He had an American Ninja style obstacle course set up in his backyard. Water pits, giant wooden structures, plus equipment designed to enhance endurance, strength, speed, and even musculature.

"This looks intense." And frightening. I wasn't twenty-five anymore. Not that I'd done anything like this when I was in my twenties or any other age.

He shrugged and crossed his arms, looking me over, which gave me a chance to admire his masculine beauty. The corner of his mouth lifted slightly as he spoke. "We have to hone your strength and show you how *not* to use it."

"Not?"

"If a baby is trapped under a car, it's okay to lift the car. People will credit adrenaline. If you drop a quarter under the car, even though you can lift it, a passing human might freak out a little if you've got it propped in one hand while you feel around for the quarter with the other." He lifted a brow.

Okay so that made sense.

I nodded, clapped my hands together and rubbed. "Lead on, Miyagi."

He turned to look. "What?"

I chuckled. "Not big on the pop-culture, huh?"

"No." He stared at me for an explanation.

I could've explained it, maybe even suggested a viewing one night soon, but by the time the thought came to me, he moved on. "The fence protects the neighbors from the lights." He pointed to the corners where floodlights were installed on poles that lit the entirety of the massive yard.

"Why didn't you just get a place outside the city? A place where you could light up the world and not worry about bothering anyone." The houses on this street weren't particularly close together, but the house wasn't solitary, either. Eventually, there would be noise complaints. Especially after my first whoop of success.

"This is close to the city for the club, and there isn't much of a food supply for us out in the wilderness."

True. Unless he liked bunnies.

About forty minutes into vampire fight club, where Jax taught me how to disappear into the shadows and move fast enough to avoid his equally fast jabs, Ransom showed up, and we worked the obstacle course. I was fast. So fast I was a blur, even to me.

The action was the most exhilarating thing I'd ever done. I moved instinctually, my body automatically knowing where to go and when. Running, being fast, it was like magic. Was this my power?

By the end of the training, I could throw, quickly fade into the shadows, put the end of a dart through the eye of a needle—literally—and I could almost harness and restrain enough strength not to make a human look twice.

It was around four when Luke showed up. He knocked on the front door, and even though we were in the backyard, we all heard it. Ten years ago, when I was the queen of gossipy book clubs—I'd belonged to three back then—hearing like this would've been so useful.

Jax answered the door and brought him around back. Luke waved. "Hey, all."

I wasn't sure when I'd been relegated to "all," but I smiled at him anyway. Not that he noticed since he was busy batting his eyelashes at Ransom, and it became clear why I was now a part of the "all."

"What's up?" I moved closer to him.

"I came bearing gifts." He smiled down at me, empty-handed.

"Okay." I chuckled. "Are you hiding them?"

He laughed when I squinched my brow. "I didn't

know you wouldn't be home. Your rock and roll all night status is new, and I'm not quite used to your hours."

He had showered and smelled like he'd spritzed on more than one squirt of cologne. Then again, that could've been my new vampire senses intensifying the scent. His shiny shoes and ironed shirt said he'd spent some time on his wardrobe. He always had.

I didn't mention it, though. That wouldn't have been sisterly. I didn't want him to point out that after working out, I probably looked like a dishrag.

"Sorry. Lead on, big brother."

On the way out of the back yard and across the street, Luke managed to position himself next to Ransom, who kept his side of the conversation to monosyllabic answers.

I unlocked the door, and we all filed in. Entertaining vampires was much easier than humans; I didn't have to offer food or drinks. I didn't miss any of the conversation for it, either.

Luke handed me a basket roughly the size of a hat box. "Ta-da!" He yanked the towel covering it off with an arm flourish that only he or Vanna White could make look regal and not ridiculous. The basket was full of donor bags of blood. "I figured it was like Snickers bars for you now."

"Oh, my." I mentally added Snickers to the list of things I would miss, then smiled at Luke. He really was a good brother. I loved him. "Thank you, but...how?"

"Girl! You remember Mark? The guy who thought every single day was an episode of Survivor?" I didn't, but nodded because Luke's explanations were only going to get more drawn out. "He works at a blood bank."

Jax shook his head. "A blood bank?" I could see the red flag in his mind. Everyone in a ten-mile radius could see the red flag. Everyone but Luke. "You told him about vampires? About us?"

Luke cleared his throat and shook his head. "No. Of course not. I have a personal relationship with Mark." Jax cocked an eyebrow, but Luke waved him off and continued. "He asked why I needed the blood. I didn't answer right away. After a bit, he admitted he already knew about vampires."

Jax's anger was visual—pinched face, narrow eyes, tight line of his lips. The only thing missing was an angry growl.

Luke was still oblivious. "He said he dated a vampire several years ago. Then said something about the vampires trying to compel him to forget about them, but he has a natural resistance to mind control or something like that." Luke looked at Jax, then to me.

Jax breathed in deeply through his nose, which was a total man-move because vampires didn't really need to breathe. He looked at me. "It isn't common knowledge that vampires exist. Not since the hunters supposedly took out the last one."

I didn't know the hierarchy or the lore, or even this history.

Jax leaned against my couch. "Our king is married to a witch who cleans up when someone finds out we're still around who shouldn't have. Do we need to make the call?" He turned to Luke and stared, eyebrow cocked.

"No." I stepped between them and glared at Jax. "Luke said Mark knows. If a vampire tried to compel him, surely you would have known about this."

Ransom nodded. "I remember Mark now. He dated a vampire from another clan that was visiting the area and decided to stay. Adam something. When Adam found his true mate, Paige and I went to wipe Mark's memories. That man has a strong mind. We couldn't take all the memories from him."

Jax relaxed. "This is the same guy?"

Ransom bobbed his head up and down. "Yep. Worked at a blood bank."

Jax gave my brother a hard look. "You got lucky, then. Mark is a trusted human. He is sworn to secrecy. Just as you should be."

Luke pressed his hand to his hips. "I would never do anything to hurt my sister. I was trying to be helpful, especially after what happened at the club tonight."

Jax whirled around to face me. "What happened?"

I scrunched up my face at his tone, then glared at my big mouthed brother. Before I could explain, Ransom cut in. "Grey happened, but Hailey handled him perfectly."

Laughing at Ransom's grin, I briefly explained what happened, and that I compelled him. By the time I finished, Jax was laughing. "I guess we don't have to worry about Grey being a problem anymore."

There was a story there, but I decided to ask about it later. I could feel the sun coming up and all my energy draining with it.

## CHAPTER EIGHT

The night shift at Cleo's started at eight and ran until Tracy finished with her late evening study group. It wasn't much, but I needed the money. Despite Jax's informal request not to go, and his modest pouting, I went anyway.

Cleo was sympathetic. "Was the accident horrible?"

I hated lying, so I kept things vague. "Definitely unexpected."

The sweet woman patted my hand. "Your friend didn't explain your injuries."

"It was nothing, really. A couple of bumps. A bruise or two." I sat in the chair beside her bed, hoping I wasn't being obvious about lying. Cleo was smart, but I didn't know if she knew about vampires or the paranormal and I wasn't going to tell her. "I think I had more internal injuries than external because I slept a lot for the first few days." There, a half-truth because I did sleep for four days.

She furrowed her brow. "But you feel okay now?"

I nodded. "I feel great. Ready to go back to work because sitting around the house is driving me crazy."

Cleo laughed. "Tell me about it. I'm itching to go back to work. If you ask me, physical therapy is moving too slow. Don't even get me started on how Tracy is babying me."

Relieved to finally have the conversation shift, I took the chance to switch the topic around to bounty hunting. "How does it work? Your job. I know the basics because my ex-husband was one, but we really didn't go into the details. I mostly did research for him."

I couldn't ask him directly. That was a call I dreaded. He'd want to come for a visit, see the house, and all that jazz. He always knew when I was lying or hiding something. So, avoidance was the key when it came to Howard. He couldn't come visit me under any circumstances.

She shrugged and motioned to herself, propped

in her bed. "It's dangerous. But it's also exciting and adventurous." She giggled. "I went on a date a while back and you should've seen his eyes when I told him I once tracked a skip to Colorado and chased him down a mountain on skis while he shot at me and everyone else on the bunny slope."

She shook her head and smiled. The memory was obviously a fond one. "It was treacherous. And once, I was shopping for groceries at the Bargain Bagger, and I saw my skip walking through the store like she was queen of produce. I yelled, 'Stop! I command you in the name of the law!' She threw a grapefruit at me, so I chased her through the dry goods and tackled her at the deli. The secret was keeping my body between her and the exit. So long as she couldn't get past me, there was nothing stopping me from picking up that collection fee."

This was a woman who was proud of her accomplishments. It reflected in her dark brown eyes as she told the stories.

I could do all that, especially since I was a new brand of invincible and immortal. My training with Jax was helping. After one night, I was already faster, and my reflexes were off the charts. It was so cool.

She yawned a couple of times, so I stood and collected an empty glass from the end table. "You are a woman who knows her business. I'm going to let you sleep now, and we can talk more the next time I'm here."

She nodded, and I helped her move down deeper into her bed. "I'm glad you came back, Hailey."

"I'm glad, too," I whispered.

I flicked off her bedroom light, then shut the door most of the way so the light from the living room wouldn't bother her.

Tracy came home around one-thirty, but I was glad for any time I could work.

She smiled as she hung up her jacket. "How was she tonight? She's been a little moody, kind of depressed. She hates not being able to get out there and track skips and nabbing perps and all that other bounty hunter jargon she's always grumbling about."

"She's good. We talked for a bit then she went to sleep." I couldn't imagine being laid up in bed. "How's her therapy going so far?"

Tracy shrugged, then crossed her arms, rubbed her biceps, and looked at the door to her mother's room. "She's trying, but she gets so unhappy when she realizes it's going to be a while before she's out on the street again making money."

I totally understood that. "She'll get there. I can also help with the therapy if you like. You know, get her up and walking more. I might make it a challenge for her. She seems like the type that loves to be challenged. Lying in bed is not helping her."

Tracy's eyes brightened. "Sure, that would be great, as long as she doesn't overdo it."

"I'll make sure she doesn't." I picked up my bag from the end of the sofa. "I'll see you later."

"Bye and thanks."

When I left Cleo's apartment, I pulled my phone out to call for a ride, but Ransom was already in the parking garage waiting. Because I had to make my lie about the car accident look real, I couldn't exactly drive myself until my car was 'fixed.' That meant I couldn't drive it to work for another week or so.

After I hopped into Ransom's car, we headed straight to Catch and Release to meet Jax. He was adamant that, if I had to go to work, I would meet him to feed when I left. He was being a little over-protective since the Grey incident, even though I'd handled myself quite well. Plus, I was hungry, which wasn't anything really new, it was just a stronger urge since I had only had a sip from the blood basket when I woke this evening.

When I'd had a nice long drink, I found Jax. "Can I catch a ride home with you? Ransom brought me here, but he's occupied again." I glanced at the bar where Ransom was washing glasses while talking to Luke.

"Sure." His deep, smooth voice washed over me. I ignored the shiver of awareness, the tremble when I was near him. We'd spent so much time together lately, I should've been immune, but the man was potent in the way chocolate had been before I was bitten.

We walked out to his car, and he drove us toward home while I tried to think of things to talk about that weren't my training or my hunger for the red stuff.

Fortunately, the ride wasn't long, so I pretended to sing to the radio when no topics for chit chat came to mind. It wasn't until he pulled onto our road that I saw the one thing that made my stomach clenched like a cramp. *Brad.*

Well, not him actually. His car and the fact that he was not *in* his car meant he was in *my* house. And how the hell had he gotten in? I had to install a better lock on the door.

The last person in this world I wanted to see was Brad, especially while I was pale faced and still dressed for work.

What the hell was he doing here? Did the home-wrecker kick him to the curb already?

Because Jax noticed everything, he glanced at me. "You okay?"

Big fat liar that I was, I nodded. "Right as rain."

Speaking of which, I turned in the car to face him and to stall. "Can I go out during the day on rainy days?"

He shook his head. "Better not. UV rays are not our friends. Besides, then you'll get your sleep schedule all screwed up. You don't want that."

"No, I guess not." I missed seeing people in the morning, all dressed for work, ready to take on a new day. The only people I saw these days were Jax and his brother and Kendra and mine. Although, seeing Cleo and Tracy was nice.

What I didn't want was to go into the house and talk to Brad, but I couldn't say anything because I didn't want Jax to know my ex was here. Not because he would care, but because I was embarrassed to admit the guy that I hadn't been enough for was inside my dang house. He would ask why, then I would have to answer, and nothing was worse than pointing out my own flaws.

"You want to train for a while?" Jax asked.

Yes. I did. But I couldn't because... Brad. I faked a yawn I didn't feel. "I'll probably turn in early today.

First day back at work..." Faked another yawn. "So tired."

If he didn't know I was a liar, he had very low standards for actors. But he nodded, smiled his pretty smile, and climbed out and walked toward his front door. I got out and stood for a couple of seconds watching, because that man had a stride worth noticing.

He disappeared inside his house, and I took a deep breath—for courage—then hurried to my front door. Brad, stretched on the sofa with his shoes on the cushion, snorted a short snore. I could've eaten him. No one would've known. Except me, and probably Jax who wouldn't be too impressed with my self control. Or probably with my selection of dinner menu.

Although, I was pretty fast now. I could bury the body before anyone saw. But I wasn't great at lying. I wonder if Jax would help me with acting lessons.

Instead of killing the cheating good for nothing jerk, I stood over him. Hmm. I thought about eating him for another second, but there were better uses for this one. He was a prime candidate for me to practice my compulsion techniques. A bonus on the front and back end. Front end—practice, back end, I could convince him to go away and never return.

I woke him by shoving his shoe-clad feet to the floor a little rougher than I'd intended because I had vamp strength now.

He startled awake and sat straight up. When he saw me, he gave me a crooked smile. "Hey, babe."

Ugh. I'd never liked that he called me babe instead of my name. It sounded so smarmy.

"Brad." I sat on the coffee table in front of him, looked deep into his eyes and blanked my mind. "You need to move on with your life."

He didn't blink. I had him. "Get over me and be glad I'm happy now."

But he shook his head and his brow wrinkled while he smirked. "What the hell are you talking about? I'm not here because I haven't moved on with my life. I'm here to check on you. Make sure you're not falling apart."

Smug bastard thought I was falling apart? That I needed checking up on? I should've eaten him. But more than annoyed, why hadn't the compulsion worked? It worked at the club with Grey.

"What are you doing here?" I asked, exasperated.

He'd already explained, but as much as I wanted to be a bad mamajamma who wasn't bothered by my ex showing up—the same ex who'd left me at the altar—he was the reason I'd moved here in the first place. Seeing him at the hospital was too much. Then the random appearances at my place had started, and I had to get out of there.

Now he was here. Please, God tell me he hadn't moved to Philly.

Before I could make my repulsion known, the door burst open and Jax stood in the living room. His eyes flashed, then went dark. Deathly dark. "What in the hell is going on here?"

Oh, holy crap, that was the hottest entrance I'd ever seen. But Brad, being the overstuffed jerk he was, looked up at Jax. "WTF, man?" Yeah. He was the kind of guy who said WTF. He looked at me in indignation. "Who the hell is this guy?"

"Who the hell are *you*?" Jax wasn't giving up information, not because he was private. He was. Not because we didn't have anything to hide. We did. But because he had this whole mystery man vibe, and he was sticking to it.

"I'm her fiancé."

"*Ex*-fiancé," I said fiercely. It was a small correction, but important to me.

Jax made a sound from low in his chest that rumbled in his throat.

Brad pulled his head back and widened his eyes. "WTF, dude. Did you just growl?"

And when the heck did the word *dude* make its comeback? Was I so old I missed it? When had Brad turned into such a douche?

"I'll show you growling!" Jax roared, but I put a hand up to stop him. To his credit, he froze and glowered.

"Hey, could we all put our dicks away and stop trying to measure whose is bigger?" I asked. That was mostly meant for Brad, who always had to be the biggest turd in the room.

But the fool advanced, and Jax cocked his head in a come-and-get-it silent dare.

"Stop!" I stepped in front of Brad and glared. I *definitely* should've midnight-snacked him when I had the chance. "Knock it off."

Then I glanced at Jax and kept my voice low. "Can't you just compel him already? I tried and can't for some reason."

His lip curled in a sneer and his voice stayed low and grumbly. "Gladly."

The growl, like everything else, was sexy enough that I cocked my head. A lesser woman would've pictured him naked. I wasn't lesser, but I was lesser enough to picture him shirtless.

"Tell him to move on with his life and forget me, to think of me fondly, but to move on." Way on. Like into the next life on.

Jax shot me a glare. "I'd rather just eat him."

Yep, me too. But that would've just caused more questions.

I rolled my eyes. His metaphorical dick was still out, and I shot him the girlfriend glare—even though I wasn't his girlfriend. It worked. He spoke softly to Brad, then led him to the door. When they stopped so he could push Brad out, Brad turned, hand extended. "Hailey, I'm so glad to see you happy. It's all I've ever wanted for you."

To my credit, I didn't vomit. I shook his hand instead. Then he turned to Jax.

"You, my man, thank you for taking care of her." He shook Jax's hand and looked at me again. "I think I can move on now. This feels like good closure."

Jax shut the door behind my ex, hopefully for the last time.

Blech. I should've gotten points for not eating him, but since Jax hadn't smiled in a little while, I kept my opinion to myself until he turned to me. He whirled around and glared at me. "Going to bed early?" He faked a yawn, imitating me, and added a ridiculous and awkward stretch that irritated me, because I'd done the move in front of him, and now I knew what it looked like.

I rolled my eyes again, then stalked to my room. He could damn well show himself out. I was tired of it all. I especially didn't want to talk about Brad to Jax.

# CHAPTER NINE

Sunset wasn't a time when I'd usually enjoyed coffee, but at least I could drink it. If I mixed a few tablespoons of blood in, it was absolutely delicious. I didn't care if the caffeine didn't affect me like it used to. I loved the rich aroma and bittersweet taste.

I was in the middle of my second sip when I heard footsteps outside. With my coffee in hand, I went to the door and opened it before Jax could knock. His sexy smirk told me he wasn't surprised that I'd known he was there. But he wasn't alone.

Paige was with him, and she seemed anxious about something. Umm, that couldn't be good. "What's up?" I stepped back so they could come in.

Paige paced my front porch, distracted, worried, and completely oblivious to her surroundings.

"What's her problem?" I crossed my arms and watched her closely. She was much older than me so I was sure I couldn't take her. For that reason, I hoped it wasn't me that pissed her off.

Paige stopped and glared at me for a second before pacing again. "*Her* can hear just fine. My problem is that Zara has a bounty on her head." She stopped pacing again and shook her head. "It's a big bounty."

"So?" Wait, had her bounty grown? "I know she has a bounty. That was why I went after her. Granted, I didn't know at the time she was a vampire."

Paige snarled, fisted her hands, and Jax held his hand up to stop her. "It's better if we discuss this inside."

"Sure." I stepped aside again for them to enter. After making sure no one else was heading over, I closed the door.

Jax went to the kitchen, so I followed, leaving Paige to stew in the living room. He poured himself a cup of coffee and turned to face me. "Zara had a human bounty when she was human. Now, the council has put their own bounty on her."

Paige entered the kitchen and turned her nose up at the coffee. "We're going to be overrun with our kind. Not to mention the human bounty hunters out to collect. More humans and more money-hungry vamps can only mean mayhem or more vamps like you turned because they don't know who they're really going after."

Ah, yeah, I could see where that would be a problem.

Jax, on the other hand, sat down at my kitchen table and picked up the paper. He was calm, like he didn't have a care in the world. "I'm not surprised. Trying to kill a human is big business. Zara should never have been made to begin with. They'll want her to answer for what she did to Hailey. That is, if Hailey is the only one she tried to kill."

Paige wrinkled her brow and sat in the chair across from Jax.

My mind kept churning over the words 'big bounty.' I could use the money, big or not. Jax pulled a sheet of paper from his pocket and handed it to me. I read over the bond intake form and my mouth fell open. "A hundred grand? I'm in!" No hesitation.

Jax shook his head. "Oh, hell no. Too dangerous."

"You're not the boss of me." I didn't know if that was true or not, but he damned sure wasn't in my own house. I'd been running my own life for about fifteen or so years without help from anyone else. No way was I giving up that independence now. "I'm in."

Besides, I wanted a cut of that money.

He rolled his eyes, and I wasn't sure what it meant. Neither did I care because I was an adult. With superpowers. And fangs! I could do as I darn well pleased.

I could tell he wasn't going to budge on his *hell,* not without a fight. I stared down my maker. "I went after her the first time because I needed the money. That hasn't changed. Especially now that my full-time job is a part time job. But I like Cleo, who happens to be a bounty hunter. My first husband was also one, and I learned a few things from him."

Jax shook his head, but Paige stared at me, slightly nodding as if she was forming a plan. Could she be on my side with this?

Tapping her fingers on the table, Paige said, "You know, she could help."

"No. It isn't safe." Jax took a sip of his coffee and glared at his head enforcer.

"Even you have to admit her training is going far better than any newbie you've trained. She's quick and learns just as fast. She doesn't have to take the case on her own. I'll be there." Paige sat back in the chair looking a little more relaxed.

When Jax didn't reply right away, Paige added, "Besides, if you contact the council and tell them that you have a team on it, they will be less likely to interfere or send their own team. It buys us time."

Frowning, I wondered why we'd need to buy time, but I didn't ask. I needed this job. "Plus, I owe Zara for killing me."

The crazy bitch had taken my choices away from me. I wasn't sure I would have chosen a life as an immortal vampire. I wasn't sure I *wouldn't* have either. However, I wouldn't give it back now.

A few long moments later, Jax blew out a breath. "Fine. But I'm on the team as well." He pointed at me with a serious master vamp look. I was betting that was the same as a mom or dad stare.

"You will not go after her alone. We plan everything out. No one takes unnecessary risks."

"Agreed!" Anything to get him to let me participate.

They left soon after that, and I did a happy dance in the middle of the living room. I was going after Zara with vampire backup. It was me she had tried to kill, after all. I knew just the witch to add to the team. A magical boost to add to the vampire strength would be the cherry on top.

As I walked from my yard to Kendra's, my cell chirped. Luke. "Hello, big brother," I greeted.

"Don't you just sound bright eyed and sparkly fanged." He chuckled at his own joke, tiny as it was. "I have some more blood for you."

Never bad news. "Thanks!"

"I could drop it by."

"Sounds good." That also sounded like an unfinished thought. I didn't have to guess the rest of the idea.

"Maybe you can invite your neighbors? The heartthrobs without hearts?" He loved his plays on words.

"I'm on my way to Kendra's. I'm going to go after a vampire who has a bounty on her head." I grinned, barely holding onto my excitement.

I could practically hear his eyes lighting up. It sounded an awful lot like a half-squeal-half-gasp. "I want to go."

A bit like a begging five-year-old, too.

As much as I loved my brother, I loved him too much to risk his safety. "I'm a vamp, Kendra's a witch. On the food scale, we're right below gods. You're just above mosquito and roadkill."

It wasn't the kindest way to put it, but I needed him to understand I couldn't compromise his safety.

"That's why I would be the perfect bait." Before I could reply, and apologize for hurting his feelings, he hung up, and I sighed.

I wouldn't be hearing the end of this one for a while. But once I captured Zara, I could buy him something nice—a car, maybe—and he would forgive me.

I walked into Kendra's house and found her lounging on the sofa in pajamas with that Brad Pitt vampire movie on the TV and a glass of wine on the table next to her. She nodded toward the TV. "I was in the mood to interview a vampire. Seemed fitting given how your life has gone recently."

Ignoring her joke, I plopped down. "We're going to work." I filled her in on the bounty. "What do you think?"

"With your super-strength and my spells, we'll have that undead freak picked up in enough time for you to climb into your coffin before the sun barbecues your behind." She tossed her blanket away, clicked off the TV, and downed her glass of wine.

I held up my hands. "Before we get too involved with planning, I agreed to allow Jax and Paige to be on the team. Jax is being weirdly overprotective, and

Paige seems to have a score to settle. Or she just wants to catch Zara before the town is overrun with other vampires and humans trying to collect the bounty." I sat down and took a breath.

"No problem," Kendra started, then added, "I can pack some things up and we can go over there to fill them in and come up with a plan. I'll get dressed!"

We packed a bag with rooster toes and eye of newt. Kendra's enhanced spells—she'd been doing research on amplifying spells for vamps—would find Zara, slow her down and disable her, while I swooped in with the enchanted cuffs—who knew?—and together we would haul this big baddy in.

As we were about to head over to Jax's house, the doorbell rang, and she looked back at me. Of course, I knew who it was. I could smell him. But she peeked out the peephole, then turned to gape at me. "You invited Luke?"

I shook my head. "Invited is not the word I would use. I actually told him no, after I filled him in about the situation." I should have kept my mouth shut. I sighed. "Might as well let him in. He won't go away otherwise."

From outside, he said, "She's right. I won't."

She yanked the door open, and he held out a

brown paper bag with a fast-food logo on the side to her and a small donor bag of B-positive to me.

I took mine and she took hers and he breezed in. I loved the smell of crispy, golden fries, and I sniffed the air over her bag. "God, I miss food."

"Shouldn't you burst into flames for saying the Big Guy's name?" He cocked a brow at me and stood back a step as if he expected it still to happen.

I huffed out a fake sigh. "Do I look charbroiled to you?"

He laughed. "You look like vampire Rambo."

I had on a camo jacket and jeans. Kendra was dressed all in black. The nights were chilly in Chestnut Hill, and I needed to look the part, as if the weather affected me, at least.

"What are you doing here?" I added just the perfect amount of boredom into my tone. "I didn't invite you."

"Can't stop me, either." If there was a single word to describe Luke, it was *saucy,* and he lived it.

He was right. Short of using the enchanted cuffs on him, there wasn't much we could do to keep him from following and screwing everything up. Maybe I could get Ransom to distract him long enough for Kendra, Paige, Jax and me to slip out.

I glanced at Kendra. She gave a slight eye roll,

and I nodded. "Fine. You can go, but you're not getting a cut of the money."

"Fine." His smile widened. "Let me earn my Ransom. Can you imagine his face when I tell him that little old mortal me caught a big vampire escapee?"

I didn't correct his classification of Zara. I had more important things to do, like figure out how to find this chick.

We were about halfway out the door when Kendra snapped her long fingers. "Oh, Hails! Remember that room where she left us to die?"

It wasn't an image I was likely to forget no matter how old I lived to be. "Yeah."

"I found a necklace there. I kept it. I'm positive it's not yours. I bet it belonged to Zara. We could use it in the locating spell."

There were days luck shined on me, which was fair since the sun could never touch my skin again. This was one of those days.

# CHAPTER TEN

A few minutes later we were in Jax's dining room with Kendra's witch paraphernalia spread out on the table. The map of downtown Philly was in the center of it all. Paige and a few others stood around the table, watching. I hadn't seen Jax when we got here. According to Paige, he was in his office talking to the council.

Just as Kendra got started on the locator spell, Jax entered the dining room. Our eyes locked as he made his way to me. "Your brother is not going."

"I know that. He's a stubborn ass who wants to be a part of the action." I glanced at Luke at the same time Ransom came in. A smile tugged at my lips. "Maybe Ransom can be Luke's distraction."

Jax's lips twitched. "That can be arranged."

"Got her." Kendra smiled and pointed at the map. "Downtown. Near the club circuit."

Of course. It would be an ideal hunting ground for a rogue vamp. Lots of alleys and a smorgasbord of victims.

Jax pointed at Nash and Grim. "You two start at the north end of the circuit. Paige, Hailey, and Kendra will start at the south. Ransom and Luke will stay here with me and the others."

Luke opened his mouth to protest, but Ransom grabbed his hand and pulled him down a hallway. "We have more important things to do."

I heard something about research and giggled. If it hadn't been for Ransom, Luke would have had a fit about being stuck back at the home base.

Paige grabbed a pair of keys from a hook on the wall beside the garage door. "Come on. Let's go get the bitch."

Kendra and I rushed out the door after the head enforcer. I stopped short when I saw a shiny red sports car. I didn't know brands, but I knew darn well that thing cost more than my annual salary when I worked at the hospital.

Once we climbed in, Paige took off down the

street, tires squealing as she took the corners. I laughed all the way while Kendra looked a little green.

At least we didn't have to worry about getting pulled over. Paige would just compel the officer to forget he saw us.

We hit the first club on the street. Club 36. I didn't know what the number was about, but the entire place was strobe lights, loud music and grinding hips. My sensitive vampire hearing was begging me to leave. The music in combination with the people inside the club yelling over it hurt my ears.

Paige slipped something into my hand and leaned in to speak into my ear. "These will protect your hearing from the club noise and serve as a radio."

"Oh cool. Thanks!" I opened my hand to see tiny earpieces. When I slipped them into my ears, I sighed in pleasure. The music was silenced to a tolerable level.

Zara's scent filtered through the crowd, and I snarled. I'd know that scent anywhere. "She's here."

Paige and Kendra asked at the same time, "You sure?"

Their voices came through the earpieces like stereo. "Yeah. I'll never forget that cheap knock-off perfume she wore when she killed me."

I followed her scent to the back of the club with Paige and Kendra on my heels. We found her with her head buried in the neck of some poor sap who probably thought he was getting lucky but was likely one or two breaths from death already.

She looked up, and our gazes connected. I glared at her, wanting to knock that smug look off her face. She knew as well or even better than we did that while inside a club with so many humans our hands were tied. Kendra couldn't throw a spell, and I couldn't use my vampire speed or strength to get to her. Because we were law-abiding vampires.

Zara, not so much, because she took off at vamp speed. She wasn't at all worried that the guy whose neck she was sucking on was about to bleed out on the floor or that people could see her vamping.

Freaking great.

I stopped and healed the bite mark then knelt in front of him. "You're feeling ill. You must've eaten some bad chicken. Go home, drink a sports drink and rest. You'll feel better in the morning."

Kendra and Paige stood around me so the crowd

wouldn't gather. Through our earpieces, Paige gave orders to Nash and Grim.

By the time I finished making sure the rogue's victim would live, Zara was gone. I glanced at Kendra. The three of us hurried out of the club at human speed, but the rogue skip was nowhere to be found. It was like she'd vanished into thin air.

I looked at Kendra. "Did we bring the necklace? The map?"

She shook her head. "Sorry."

It wasn't her fault any more than it was mine. "No big deal. We'll head back and try again."

Although, it was getting late. Dealing with my brother and his antics and filling our supply bag, scrying for Zara's location, then finding her in the crowd, had all taken longer than I realized. But the sun was about an hour from rising.

Boy, was I feeling it.

As we pulled into Jax's driveway the front door opened and Jax and Luke rushed out.

Jax opened my door and pulled me out. "What happened?"

"She got away." I was too tired to explain and hungry. I hadn't eaten all night except for one blood bag with my evening coffee.

I turned and walked across the street to my house, hoping I made it inside before I dropped into a vamp coma.

"Hailey, stop!"

I did, but only after I got my door open. Jax crossed the space between in a flash. I looked up into his eyes and gave a weak smile. "We failed. I failed. She got away. But can we talk about it later tonight? I need to eat before the sun comes up."

Jax motioned for me to go inside. When I did, he followed, closing the door behind us. "Why haven't you eaten?"

"Forgot?" I walked to the refrigerator and pulled out a couple of blood bags. "You guys came over with the news about Zara, and I got distracted wanting to catch her."

I popped the bag into my mouth, let my fangs puncture it and blood rush into my mouth and down my throat. A sigh slipped from me as I drank.

"You shouldn't go so long without feeding." Jax leaned against my kitchen counter, watching me.

I rolled my eyes because if I removed the bag, blood would go everywhere. That would be a waste and a mess I didn't have time for.

When the bag emptied, I removed it and tossed it into the trash bin. "I said I didn't do it on purpose.

Anyway, Zara was in a human club. So, we couldn't do anything to bring too much attention. Meanwhile the rogue vamp was sucking some poor guy dry right there!"

I started to give him a play by play, but he handed me another bag. "Finish that one and go to bed. I'll get the details from Paige."

He waited for me to finish the second bag. After tossing the bag in the trash, I said. "I feel like I failed tonight. We jumped the gun a little."

"You think?" Jax's tone was teasing even though he didn't smile at me. He didn't smile a lot. Always the serious vampire master. I was learning to read his body language and his eyes to see what his mood was. Right then, he was concerned but relaxed.

"Do you feel the effects of the sun?" I asked.

His eyes snapped to mine, then he studied my face, reading me as I was him. "Not as much as you. I can stay up all day if I want to. Then again, I'm older than dirt."

I snorted then slapped my hand over my mouth while laughing. His joke had taken me by surprise. It was unexpected. When I was able to breathe without laughing, I said, "I'm sure you are not *that* old."

He smiled then, and it felt like I leveled up somehow. "Maybe not. The point is, as you age you will not be ruled completely by the sun. I can't tell you when because it's different for everyone."

I nodded, and we fell silent again. As tired as I was getting, I was enjoying Jax's company, this little bit of private time we were currently sharing. "So, what's our next step with Zara?"

"I'm not going to get you to walk away from this, am I?" he asked.

"Nope," I said, popping the *P* in the word.

He sighed and stepped closer. "I know for a fact that Paige is at home handing out assignments. At nightfall, she will have enforcers and scouts out gathering information on Zara. We need to learn her routine and set a trap."

Wow. I should hang out with Paige more often. She could teach me a few things. "Okay, so I should ask her what she needs me to do?"

Jax nodded.

After a pause, he said, "I'll give you money if you need it."

His voice was soft and gentle, but I wasn't a woman who wanted to be cared for by a man. A woman who wanted him to swoop in with his cape and fangs and bail me out of my money trouble.

"I don't want your money." There was a sharpness to my tone I didn't mean. I sighed before continuing. "I'll work for my money. I've already been thinking about getting into bounty hunting and catching human skips that would be super easy now that I have all this power."

He was silent for a few long seconds. "I would be okay with that." Softer, almost in a whisper, he added, "But I still want to give you some money. To tide you over."

"Jax..." I didn't want to sound ungrateful. "Why? Why would you want to give me money?" Then it occurred to me. "Because you made me?"

He nodded once. "As your sire, I'm obligated to take care of you."

At least he took his obligations seriously. Even if a part of me had hoped he was doing it out of concern. "I'm an adult, Jax, even if I'm a baby vampire. You can help me learn how to be a vampire, but you're off the hook for everything else. Deal?"

He simply nodded, but I could tell he wanted to argue. "Deal, but only if you will agree that if you so much as get your lights shut off, I'm giving you a monthly allowance."

"Deal." An allowance? Did he think of himself as my parent?

He leaned down until we were almost nose to

nose. Did vampires ever get bad breath? Not that Jax ever would... "My obligation to you has nothing to do with being your maker."

Then he left. I stood in my kitchen breathless and confused. What the hell did that mean?

## CHAPTER ELEVEN

The sound of my phone ringing non-stop woke me from a dead sleep. Pun intended. *No, I know I haven't been asleep all day.*

Rolling over, I grabbed my phone and checked the time before even seeing who it was. 3:00 p.m. Someone had better be bleeding, or I was going to vamp out on them.

I answered because I was awake now. "Hello?"

If I sounded snippy, that was on them. As a human, I hadn't liked middle of the night calls. As a vampire whose nights came during the day, I liked them even less.

"Hey! It's me." Kendra sounded excited. Oh goody. "I've located Zara and have been checking in on her all day. Before you ask, yes, I can do that.

Anyway, she is holed up in an apartment building on Vine Street."

She sounded like she'd drank a few more than normal espressos. "If we can get there in daylight, we could catch her while she's sleeping."

"Great, but I've given up my daylight walking rights." At the moment, I was bitter about it.

"It might be worth asking Jax if it is possible for you to go out." Seriously, how much caffeine had she had?

"Fine." I growled, low and guttural, then hung up. I already knew the answer, but it really was a good opportunity to catch this rogue.

Yeah. Because talking to Jax was exactly what I wanted to do. Except it wasn't. Of course, it had to be today that we had a hard line on Zara's location during daylight hours. I had to be a vampire, so the sunlight was no longer a friend.

Some midlife this was.

I dialed Jax's number, staring at the ceiling while I waited for him to answer. Like me, he was sleeping —or should've been, but he answered right away. "Hailey? Are you okay?"

The concern in his voice touched me more deeply than I was willing to admit. I still didn't know what he meant about feeling obligated to me, and it had nothing to do with being my maker. I really didn't want to think about it too hard.

"I have a line on Zara, a place where she's staying right now. But I kind of need to go right now." In case he was confused, I added, "In the daylight. Is that possible?"

It probably wasn't. Probably being a vampire was going to cost me my portion of a hundred grand. Just another thing lost to being a creature of the night.

"Yeah. You'll need to wear long sleeves, and gloves." He paused. "Every inch of exposed skin has to be covered and shaded. Do you have a wide brimmed hat?"

"I think so." It wasn't Rose from Titanic wide, but it was fit for a Mint Julep at the Kentucky Derby.

"Get ready and I'll be there to get you shortly."

I hadn't invited him along, but I couldn't very well refuse the help, either. "Fine."

I hung up and shot a text to Kendra and Luke.

**Get ready! It's on!**

A second later my phone pinged.

**LUKE: Bitch, please! I'm already at Kendra's. You get ready!**

I yawned twice. I had become a day sleeper and it was daytime—the equivalent to three in the morning if I were still a human. I'd always been a morning person, but this was too early when I still had a few hours before the sunset.

I hurried to the closet and rooted through the boxes and bags until I found the hat. Then I rooted around for my winter gloves and other things that would cover every inch of my skin. I looked absolutely ridiculous. It beat being deep fried by the sun.

I hated answering the door when I looked like a case study from "What Not to Wear," but Jax and everyone else was going to see me soon enough.

Yet, I need not have worried because I wasn't the only vampire who needed a fashion consult. Jax stood on my covered porch wearing a cowboy hat, pants tucked into his motorcycle boots, leather gloves and a long-sleeved gray button down. "Ride 'em, cowboy!" I crowed.

It slipped out before I could censor myself.

He laughed. "Better than pan seared."

I moved back, still giggling about my outburst and his outfit. "I don't feel bad about the way I'm dressed now."

He faced me with amusement in his features. "Listen, we can be in the sun completely covered for about fifteen minutes. Less is ideal because at sixteen, even covered, the blisters come. Longer than that..." He shook his head and mimed an explosion.

"Not exactly blown apart but burst into flames. If you go out with bare skin, you have three minutes, max."

That was comforting. "You are just a ray of sunshine...er moonshine? No, that's a drink. Moonbeams."

He chuckled. "Are you done?"

"Yeah. I need coffee." I turned to the kitchen, but Jax gripped my arm and pulled me to the door.

"No time. We need to catch her while she's asleep. Plus, the caffeine doesn't affect you anymore." I hated that he was right.

We walked out of the house and ran to the SUV. The windows were tinted dark, and I sat in the back row of seats. Jax was next to me. A large black duffel sat on the passenger side of the back seat, so Jax and I were hip to hip and shoulder to shoulder.

My skin prickled, and I took a deep breath. Being so near him had dizzying effects on my body. Lord, he smelled so good. I almost leaned in for one of those long, deep inhales, but caught myself.

Paige was in the driver seat with Ransom riding shotgun. Kendra and Luke sat in the middle row and were the only two who looked normal.

I was so jealous. They were the only ones in the car not dressed like confused clowns without makeup. Kendra looked at me over her shoulder and smirked.

Another yawn fluttered out of me, and my eyelids drooped another fraction closer to closed.

Paige took off and drove straight to the apartment building. It was close to Luke's gallery, and he directed us into the hidden parking garage under the building. Smooth sailing so far.

We hit the elevator and rode up to the apartment she'd rented in her own name. Hey, I didn't say she was the smartest skip out there.

Kendra used a spell to unlock the door and we entered, silent and determined. But we could've stampeded in like the bulls in Pamplona and no one would've cared, because the place was empty. Didn't that just figure?

Because she didn't make the same mistake twice, Kendra pulled out her map of the city and the necklace before she began to scry.

When the necklace landed twice more in the same spot, Paige clicked her tongue against her teeth. "Is there a way to narrow it down? If she's here, she has to be in a different apartment."

Ransom, the man of very few words, spoke. "We could check to see if there are any vacant apartments. Maybe she uses one of those as her sleep space."

Jax nodded and slapped Ransom on the shoulder as he walked back into the room from wherever he'd been searching. "Right. She's new, so she'll be tired."

I could testify to that and swallowed another yawn only for it to escape a second later.

"Easier to sneak up on," Jax said as he eyed me.

I went to the kitchen. There were times a girl needed to just act for herself. This was one. I needed caffeine, and I wasn't leaving without it. It didn't matter if it didn't work on me like it did when I was human. I had to try.

I rifled through the cabinets until I found a collection of coffee pods to fit in the machine next to the stove. I walked over and clicked it on.

"What are you doing?" Jax's voice, gentle and kind, on any other occasion would've elicited some not so annoyed response, but fatigue made me grouchy.

"I'm making coffee." To my credit, I didn't add *Einstein.*

"For whom?" Who did he think?

"For me. You wouldn't let me make any at the house, and I figured we had a few minutes to kill." I raised a brow at him, and he just shook his head as he walked off.

Kendra hung up her phone. "All right. They have two units open. One on the top floor, and one just above the garage on the ground floor, which is actually just below the ground. No windows. Much cheaper than this baby, let me tell you."

"That's gotta be it." I said as I came out of the kitchen with a travel mug I'd found in the cabinet full of rich, sweet, *amazing* coffee.

As a group, more like a stampede than like a bunch of covert bounty hunters trying to sneak up on a skip, we filed into the elevator, and I leaned my head back against the wall and didn't move until the doors opened and we started into the downstairs hallway.

Kendra led because she knew the apartment number and because she had to unlock the door. But we might have just as well stayed upstairs since this place was empty, too.

The ride to the penthouse was longer, and because I was so mercifully still, I snoozed a bit, until Jax nudged me with his elbow. "Are you seriously sleeping standing up?"

He was losing his hotness factor in the daylight. "I'm an infant. We need our sleep."

He chuckled, and I let my eyes fall shut again. The beauty, aside from resting, was my body continued taking unnecessary breaths, and with each one I got a big whiff of Jax. There were benefits to having him along.

When Kendra opened the door, we spread out in the apartment and Jax waved me over when he opened a closet door. There she was. Sleeping like a mean-ass rogue baby. Blanket over her. Hair splayed on the pillow like she had a lover coming to wake her and she wanted to be beautiful.

"How do we get her out of here?" It was a reasonable question, but Kendra gave me a side-eye.

"Concealment spell. We went over this, Hails."

"Infant with zero memory," I snarled, amending the description of myself for Jax's benefit because my need for caffeine or sleep overpowered my kindness gene.

Zara jerked awake and stared up at us from one to the next, because we were all in her sleeping space, and it was probably a bit startling. When she got to me, she smirked. "I thought I killed you."

I growled, and Jax put a calming hand on my shoulder. "I saved her. You *almost* killed her."

She sighed. "Sorry about that."

No, she wasn't. I narrowed my eyes. "Worst. Apology. Ever."

It was like she didn't give a damn that she ruined all my bucket list plans. No vacation in Cabo so a cabana boy could rub lotion on my back. No hike through the Grand Canyon. No Teacup ride or stay at the Cinderella castle. She was lucky I didn't stake her and take my chances with landing on someone else's skip list.

"Right?" Luke sidled closer to me and threw a protective arm around my shoulders. "You're going down, girl. No one messes with my sister and gets away with it."

"Come on. I would like to get back to bed sometime today." I wanted to cuff her and drag her out into the sunlight, but probably only because I was so tired. Maybe, once I had a nap, I might've been kinder.

Jax shot me a questioning glance with a scrunched brow and pinched lips. I shrugged and yawned.

We brought her to the car unhindered by human or vampire involvement. Considering the bounty on Zara's head, that was quite the feat, in my opinion, which no one seemed to care about since they all wanted to throw questions at Zara. They essentially each asked the same question—Why?—in different words.

She slumped, defeated. "I was bitten, turned, then left alone. Abandoned. I didn't know what to do. I was scared and so hungry." Hell, right then she was licking her lips and eyeing Luke's throat like it was T-Bone. She snapped out of it when I poked her and glared. "I don't want to kill anyone again. I know it's not right, but I can't fight it."

Bloodlust. That was the only explanation I could come up with. Jax had told me that was how most vamps turned rogue. They gave into the hunger and fed so much that they became addicted to the blood and the kill.

Even though she didn't say as much, I knew it was true. So did Jax. I glared at Zara again. Jax was my maker, and I wasn't in the mood to share with her. She could tough it out or find someone else, and damned sure, she could stop watching him with all that blatant interest flickering in her eyes.

Paige pulled the SUV into my driveway. Thankfully, the sun was low in the sky. I ditched the hat and Jax nodded. "I'll take her back with me. I have a dungeon I can keep her in."

Of course. What vampire master wouldn't be

complete without a dungeon. "What now? You have a what?"

He laughed. "Not a dungeon exactly. Just a light tight place where I can keep baby vamps or ones who've gone rogue. As the eldest US vampire—"

"I thought you said you weren't an elder." I was sure he'd told me that.

"I'm not an elder. I'm the eld*est*." A distinction without a difference? But no. "Elders are the...council, for lack of better word. I'm the oldest vampire in the United States, so I'm in charge." When my eyes went wide, he shook his head. "There aren't that many of us left in the states. We're international...more European since that TV show came out and every American with a saltshaker and silver cross likes the idea of Winchestering us."

American or not, I liked that he was catching up on his pop-culture references. "Oh. Still, glamorous."

"Not really. It only sounds cool that I have the title of eldest."

"So, you're the King of America? Does that make me a princess?" I was already picturing my tiara.

But he rolled his eyes. "I'll get in touch with my maker to arrange the hand-off and for the bounty."

He walked Zara from my house to his, and I

watched because tired or not, he had a walk that deserved appreciation.

Ransom and Paige turned to follow, then Luke hugged me close and said, "That is one sexy vampire."

"Yeah," I replied.

I was over this entire day. And even though I was about to be richer, it was going to have to wait until I finished my nap.

CHAPTER TWELVE

My nap took me well into Friday evening, and I woke up starving. My fangs fully out, poking into my lower lip, and I had a vague recollection of dreaming about blood. Jax had been there.

What the heck?

My stomach cramped. That was when I remembered I'd slept through Thursday night *and* all day today. I'd only had two bags of blood while talking with Jax in my kitchen. Talk about sleeping like a baby.

On that note, I needed blood. Now.

Out of habit, I reached for my glasses on the bedside table and slipped them on. Instead of becoming clearer, the world went blurry, and I took them off. Put them back on, then off again.

Holy crap, I could see. Without glasses.

I wasn't sure why I hadn't noticed before now, other than my life since turning into a vampire had been one distraction after another.

But I could see. Everything. Every speck of dust, and every fallen hair that had ever fallen from my brush to the carpet. I needed to clean, geez, but first, I needed a minute to revel in my perfect vision. 20/20 baby.

I was starving. I had just enough time to drink some of the gifted blood bags from Luke before I showered, getting ready for my shift at Cleo's.

When I finished, I sighed. I was probably going to be hungry again in an hour since I went almost a whole night without feeding. I didn't need to be tempted to suck on my patient's neck. So, I put a couple bags into a lunchbox before I left for work.

When I arrived at Cleo's, I put the bag into the fridge and went to check on her.

I knocked once and slowly opened Cleo's bedroom door. "Hey."

"You have a little something..." She swiped her finger over her own lips and when I did mine, I pulled back a smear of blood from my hand.

"Must've bit it." I averted my eyes, focusing on the carpet.

"What big teeth you have today. I hope you're not planning on eating me. I'm not Red Riding Hood." She laughed, but the humor never quite reached her eyes.

I chuckled, too, but this was as close to being discovered as I'd been, and I wasn't sure I could ensure her safety if she knew for certain what I was. But how could she possibly know what I was? Most supernatural creatures didn't even know vampires existed anymore.

I excused myself and went to the kitchen because sure enough, I was hungry already. I warmed my blood and poured it into a mug—less conspicuous, and less savage than drinking from the bag.

I caught movement from the corner of my eye and jumped when Cleo walked into the room. Hey! She was walking.

"What are you doing?" I shook my head but beamed at her. "I'm happy to see you moving, but why are you up?"

"The therapist gave me the green light. Obviously, I'm not running marathons, but..." She shrugged and moved her feet from side to side, then front to back.

"Well, now you're just showing off." My smile

this time was guarded. As happy as I was for her, I had half a mug of blood behind me.

It was a big accomplishment. A woman like Cleo—vibrant and athletic—wasn't meant to be stuck in bed recuperating. I was glad to see her up and about.

She waved her hand in front of her face. "Yeah, yeah. Enough about me. Are you a vampire?"

Holy crap. "Psh. What?" I danced from one foot to the other. "*What*? Vampire? No. No!"

"Are you lying?" She eyed the empty blood bag still on the counter. Ah, crap.

I followed her line of sight and dropped my shoulders. "Yeah. That's me being a big fat liar. How do you know about vampires?"

I thought we weren't common knowledge. The story that'd been passed around was that the supposed last vampire was killed by a hunter. Vamps had lived in secret since.

"Oh, come on. I've been around the block a time or two." When I cocked my eyebrow, she laughed. "I dated a witch once."

"Wow. The supernatural world isn't as secret as I thought it was."

"How long?" she asked.

"My 'car accident,'"—air quotes—"was more of a

blood draining, then a guy bit me to save me kind of thing."

Cleo nodded. "Yeah. You didn't look much like you'd been in an accident when you came back to work."

She was right. I looked stronger than ever.

She sat at the table, and I pulled out her stash of cookies to set them in front of her. She chewed thoughtfully. "I wondered at the change to night shifts."

"Yeah. Now, I have to find something to make up the income. I thought I would try my hand at bounty hunting." I shrugged. "Once you're on the go again, you won't need me here."

She nodded. "It's good money, and there's always some butthead who thinks he's smarter than the hunter so...steady work isn't ever an issue."

"I'm super strong now. Fast. Give me a cape, and I'm Superwoman." I flexed a deceptively pathetic-looking muscle in my arm.

I eyed my patient. "Anyway. I was thinking we could partner up. You have the connections. My friend Kendra has a serious location spell, and I have the brute strength." Not something I ever thought I would say. "What do you think? We could tackle twice the skips as a team as you can alone."

"But I would have to split the money." Cleo cocked her head as if she were thinking about it.

"But the earning potential is greater because with all three of us, we could work faster. Haul in more bail jumpers and larger bounties." I'd heard Howard use the phrase a few times.

She considered me with her head cocked. "Right now, I need the help."

I didn't nod or move. I just sat and waited with bated breath.

"All right. I'm in." She held out her hand, and I gave it a solemn shake.

With the pressure off, we sat and chatted about what it meant to be a vampire until Cleo was tired and went to bed. She was better but still not at full strength. It would take a while.

When Tracy came home, I left and headed to my neighborhood, but instead of going to my own house, I went to check in with Jax. I was thirsty and almost out of Luke's gift bags. I thought, hoped, we could head to the club for a drink.

I didn't need him going with me, but I wanted him to. He was nice to be around.

I knocked and Ransom opened the door, a pained scowl on his face. Tension rolled off him, and I frowned. Oh God. What was I walking into?

I stepped further inside, and he shut the door behind me. Jax sat stiffly on a chair opposite a man I'd never seen before. They both stood when I entered the room, old-fashioned style. The man looked Italian with dark hair and eyes. He was well built but not grossly muscular, wearing a well-tailored suit.

Paige stood on the other side of the door by Ransom, like they were on guard duty.

"Um, hi?" I wasn't usually tentative when greeting anyone, but the air in the room was tight and tense and my usually bubbly self wouldn't have fit in with this lot.

I really wanted to just leave, but I was there, and the new guy had already seen me.

Jax stared at me for a second, then extended his hand to me. "Hailey, this is Dominic." He paused for the space of a second, then lowered his voice and added, "My maker."

Dominic motioned to the seat beside Jax. "Please. Sit. Join us." He spoke in a Scottish accent. It would've been sexy if he wasn't so intimidating.

He was cool. No. He was *cold*. Very formal with a deep voice and pale, olive-toned skin. If Anne Rice based her characters on real guys, this dude was

Lestat. He reached to pick up a duffel beside his chair. "The bounty."

He tossed it so it landed between me and Jax. I looked at Jax, and he nodded like I'd asked if I could open it. If there was some sort of honor system for vampires, a trust in one another, I wasn't privy to such details yet. Nor did I care. I might have been a hundred-percent vampire, body-wise, but my trust instincts were still a hundred percent human. And American.

I pulled back the zipper, and my eyes widened. I'd never seen a hundred grand in person and had no idea how many stacks of bills it would take, but there were a *lot*. Different denominations. Stacks of tens, twenties, fifties, even some ones.

"No worries. I can get it laundered." Jax's voice was calm, like normal people sitting around in their living rooms with their makers and discussing washing the filth off duffle bags filled with cash.

I was not of the same opinion. To me it was a big deal, and I was sure my wide eyes and pinched brow said what my words didn't.

Jax cleared his throat. "How was your trip over from Scotland?"

"The air strip,"—Dominic looked at me as if I'd

asked another question. "The elders have a private air strip in Edinburgh, and we schedule flights to land after dark to avoid suspicion when we are unloaded if we travel by coffin."

His voice had the lilt of a Scotsman with a bit of an English purr. I loved accents and could recognize most. I could tell an Italian from a French, from a Spanish, from an Irish and Scottish. Sometimes, I could even mimic them if I tried hard.

But I had to say *travel by coffin* didn't sound nearly as appealing as window seats and first-class flutes of champagne. Of course, my days of flying commercial were likely over.

I nodded at Dominic as he continued speaking to Jax, but I ignored their conversation, instead adding another item to the things being a vampire had taken from me.

Dominic looked at me. "The elders thank you for your part in apprehending Zara."

I didn't know what to say so I nodded.

He shook his head. "That was a bit of distasteful business we're happy to have squashed."

Squashed? I didn't ask because Jax laid his hand over mine and gave a squeeze, then pulled away. Either he wanted me to be unable to find words because he'd touched me, thereby wreaking havoc on my thought processes, or he was trying to tell me to shut up, which he didn't have to worry about because of the first thing.

"Do you have to go back right away?" Jax spoke when my words failed. He stared at Dominic, and I wasn't sure which answer would make him happier.

Dominic shook his head. "No. I'll be staying in your quaint little town for a couple days."

Quaint little town? He sounded like a posh British ass.

Paige stepped forward. "Hailey, what do you say we go get a drink and let these guys catch up?"

"Sure." I stood and walked outside with her, glad to have the excuse to leave. Plus, my stomach was gnawing at me.

I was three steps from the curb when I realized I'd forgotten my purse. It was on the sofa next to Jax. "Hang on. I'll be right back."

I opened the door and went to get Ransom's attention but stopped when Dominic spoke. "I hope he won't be a problem."

I didn't mean to listen, but Dominic wasn't whispering, and the house had straight lines that allowed sound to carry. Especially arrogant Scottish sounds.

"No, that's all ancient history. I'm sure he's going to avoid me while he's here." Even from a room away, it was as easy to picture Jax's confidence as it was to hear it in his voice.

"Good. That's settled then."

I wondered who they were talking about, but I didn't know enough about Jax to know who or what was all ancient history.

Deciding to leave the purse, because there was no way I wanted to face Dominic again, I walked outside, unnoticed, and to the car where Paige waited to take me to Catch and Release.

As I climbed in and buckled up, Paige started the car. After she'd driven a mile or so, she spoke. "We'd hoped to get Zara out of here before Dominic learned about you."

I wasn't sure why it mattered, but she continued. "Now, we have to hope Jax can convince him to keep it quiet."

"Why?"

Paige shot me a glance. "Turning new vampires is against our laws." Jax had told me that much. "There is a process each human has to go through, and the Elders need to be aware of the potential turnee and approve them." Paige frowned.

My stomach soured. "So, Jax broke the law when he turned me."

Why would he take such a risk? Why me?

We spent long enough at the club for me to have a couple of drinks, then she dropped me at home. I wasn't in the mood for partying, just needed to feed. After unlocking my door, I stopped short when I opened it.

At first, I wondered if Brad had come back to annoy me. But it wasn't Brad sitting on my sofa. It was Dominic.

He rose grandly. "Miss Whitfield." When he added a bow, I cocked my head. "I was rather hoping you would like to go to dinner with me tomorrow night."

"Do we eat dinner?" As far as I knew we couldn't. The water I drank when I first woke as a vamp hadn't stayed down. Then again, I was now able to drink coffee.

He chuckled. "Among our kind, *dinner* is said as a polite word for hunting."

"Uh...I don't, that is, I haven't..." Hunting wasn't really something I wanted to do, but I needed to learn, I supposed. "Sure. I'd love to go to dinner with you. Tomorrow...tonight?"

*Way to show you're a newbie vamp, Hailey.*

There was no way I could go now because there was only about an hour left before sunrise.

"Splendid." He swept past me and out my front door.

Yeah. Maybe for him. He wasn't the one who had to tell his maker he was going to dinner with me.

## CHAPTER THIRTEEN

I walked into Cleo's the next night, and she was already waiting for me, a stack of pages in her hand. "I printed out some skips I think you can capture easily. They're cases I've had trouble tracking down, and they have higher payouts."

Oh, nice. "Yeah?"

I took the stack and read a few reports. There were a couple of assault suspects, a retail theft, but an assault with a deadly weapon was the one I stopped to read more completely.

The woman had a couple of kids and lived in the area. By all accounts—at least by the one who'd signed the bond sheet on the woman's behalf—this woman was a good mother.

"I don't think she would leave her kids. Doesn't

strike me as the type," Cleo said, noticing which one I was reading.

If that was the case, shouldn't she have been able to find this woman?

As if she could read my mind, she shook her head. "But I've never been able to pin her down."

"Maybe if we work together..." Kendra would need something personal of the woman's. I glanced at the paperwork. "It says they sent over her watch and cell phone?"

Cleo nodded and walked slowly into the other room, then came back a few minutes later with a plastic bag marked with the woman's name. "She was in such a rush to leave the police station so she could run out on her bond that she forgot her junk."

"Her loss is Kendra's scrying tool." I pulled out my phone called Kendra, tapping my foot as I waited for my best friend to pick up. When she did, I filled her in. "So, if you can meet us here, maybe we can track her down."

"I'll be right over," she said excitedly. "Text me the address."

When she arrived with her city map, Cleo and I sat back and watched. It didn't take long. Once Kendra had a location, I nodded at Cleo. "Isn't that just something?"

We both nodded in glee. "That witch I dated didn't know the business end of her broom." She laughed at her little play on words. "No way would she have been able to figure out this kind of magic. Didn't have any Houdini Hardware whatsoever."

I didn't bother correcting her that Houdini was a magician who relied on sleight of hand and illusion. What Kendra did was a whole other ballgame.

Cleo sat up. "Okay, you two. I'm fine here. You go get that woman and make us some money. Assault with a deadly should be about a fifteen-grand bounty. I'll take twenty percent off the top as a finder's fee."

Fine by me. We wouldn't have even thought of doing this without Cleo. Of course, if not for Cleo and this job, I'd still be human, but still.

She looked again at the address Kendra had written out. "But that's a sketchy part of Philly, so you gals are going to want to be careful."

She picked up her purse and pulled out a stun gun, a pair of cuffs, a pen light, and a pistol. I took the cuffs and Kendra took the stun gun. We ignored the actual gun.

I looked at Kendra who was already staring wide-eyed at me. "Wow. What do you think?" I was pretty excited.

She grinned. "I'm not worried. I've got a vampire guarding my body and a taser if my vamp gets lazy." She chuckled. "What do you think? Feeling strong?"

Confidence rushed through me, along with excitement and a surge of adrenaline. "I can handle myself."

Plus, I'd been training in all my overnight hours with Jax.

"All right then." Cleo nodded. "What are you waiting for? Call me when you have her in custody."

She made it all sound so easy, but I was a bundle of nervous energy. I climbed into Kendra's Prius and studied the booking sheet while she backed out and put us on the road to the address.

Cleo wasn't lying when she said the neighborhood was seedy. Broken and boarded windows were featured on every building on the street, and the graffiti on the house fronts seemed to be the new numbering system.

Kendra pulled in front of a small apartment building, shut off the car, and clenched the wheel with both hands. "We're doing this?"

"You bet we are. We're going to kick some felon bail-jumper butt." My optimism lacked the enthusiasm of true belief, but it was enough to spur her into action.

She climbed out and waited for me to gather our supplies from where we'd stowed them in the console. I handed her the taser then tucked the cuffs into my waistband, one dangling over the top.

We knocked on the apartment door and Kendra called out, "Pizza delivery."

A woman with long, curly hair pulled the door open and stood in a velvet jogging suit from a bygone era for about half a second before she tried to shut the door.

Not so fast, lady. She couldn't get it shut faster than I could move. I pushed my way in and backed her toward a disgusting gold sofa with stained cushions and a flat pillow back.

That was all it took. She sat heavily and buried her head in her hands. "How did you find me?" She huffed out a breath, and neither Kendra nor I answered. "Please. I have little kids who need me."

"You just have to go downtown and arrange for a new bond," I said. "You'll be out and able to go home by morning."

It was how Cleo had explained the process. She'd also said telling skippers how it worked sometimes was enough to convince them to come peacefully with us.

The woman sighed. "Please!" A tear slipped

down her cheek followed immediately by a flood of them. I believed her and looked at Kendra.

"Maybe we should let her go," I mouthed at my best friend.

Kendra looked sympathetic. I'd half made up my mind to pretend we'd never found this woman before she pulled a knife from between the cushions and made a wide, slicing arc through the air in my direction.

"Are you freaking kidding me right now?" I shook my head and dodged her second attempt to end me with her kitchen knife.

Not that it would end me, but it would piss me off.

She wasn't getting a third chance. I took the knife and forced her down. It was...easy. I hadn't had a chance to measure my strength against a human. Jax was stronger than me. Paige and Ransom were stronger. But no human was going to overpower me, for sure.

More than marveling at my own strength—impressive as it was—I was tired of dealing with this woman. I wanted to be finished with her, collect the bounty, and bask in the glory of it.

Without much more fanfare, we loaded the trussed-up woman into the Prius and drove to the precinct closest to the apartment building. Skips could be turned in at any station since the warrants issued were statewide.

Once I had the recovery verification slip in hand, I called Cleo. "We did it!"

"I knew you could!" Her excitement rang through the phone.

The only other thing I needed to know was where to go to collect the money. I was pretty sure we couldn't just pop into the ATM vestibule and expect a payout. "Now what do we do?"

She rattled off an address downtown. "The front door will be open, but Jordan will be asleep in the back room. Hit the bell on the counter until he comes out. He'll take care of you. Just tell him I sent you."

I didn't want to trust some random stranger with our money. Especially since it was so much. "Who is this guy?"

"Only the best in the business. He trained me." She sniffed. "Mostly, he's retired now, but he used to go after the skips, and no one *ever* got away from Jordan." There was a note of hero-worship in her voice. "He trained me to be the hunter I am today."

All right. If he was good enough for Cleo, he was good enough for me.

Kendra drove us to the address, and we walked in. The place wasn't much more than a dingy office front with giant windows next to the door that let passersby see inside. There was a wide counter with an old-style hotel bell that I slapped a couple of times.

It was quiet except for my incessant ringing, and Kendra and I looked at one another. After Cleo's high praise, I'd expected something grander, something more elegant, but this place was little better than a hole in the wall.

I'd pictured Jordan as a big, buff mountain of a man like the TV hunters. He would *have* to be super big, and super tough to earn the kind of awe I'd heard in Cleo's voice.

The back door opened, and light poured out into the front room. My nerves clenched. The moment of truth.

I couldn't stop my jaw from dropping as a teeny-tiny, half-bald man walked out. He was more leprechaun than mountain.

I cleared my throat, ready to assert myself with tone, but I squeaked because nerves behaved that way. "Jordan?"

"Who's asking?" He had a Danny DeVito as the Penguin walk and the hairline to match. His voice, though, belonged to Michael Jackson before puberty with a southern drawl.

I stepped forward, still not convinced this was the amazing bounty hunter who never lost his mark. "Cleo sent me. I'm Hailey and this is my associate, Kendra." I smiled hesitantly. "You're *the* Jordan? The one who owns the bonds office? Who trained Cleo? The best bondsman she's ever worked with?"

He put one hand on his hip. "Of course, that's me. What? Expecting Rambo?"

He probably got that reaction enough to expect it, but if so, his sharp and somewhat bitter tone said he didn't quite enjoy it.

Mini-Rambo held out his hand, and I thought he wanted to shake. I shifted the bond slip to my left hand and gave him a firm, professional shake. He rolled his eyes, then sighed. "Bond receipt?"

His accent said southern United States. Maybe Tennessee. He had an Appalachian twang.

Oh. "Sorry."

I handed it over, and he pulled out a large binder checkbook, then wrote a check. To *me*. Holy crap, I'd never made this kind of money. Not for one night of work, for sure.

"Thank you," I said. "We hope to do more business with you in the future."

Jordan waved me off, so I took the check and walked out, keeping my composure until I was around the corner then, and only then, did I dissolve into the fit of laughter that had been bubbling inside me since he'd first opened the door and stepped into the light.

Kendra leaned against me, chortling.

Fifteen grand! Now this was a payday worth working for.

## CHAPTER FOURTEEN

By the time I got home, after chasing the skip and celebrating my first takedown with Cleo and Kendra, it was too late to hunt with Dominic. I called and politely rescheduled. He was, thankfully, gracious.

When I walked out my front door Sunday night to go to work, Dominic was poised on my doorstep, hand lifted to knock. "Miss Whitfield. You look lovely. Are you ready for our hunt?"

When I'd spoken to him yesterday, I'd told him I would have to take a rain check, but I never mentioned when. Certainly, I hadn't said *tonight*. "I have to work." Cleo's daughter had a date tonight. She was trusting me. "Maybe we can go tomorrow night?"

Dominic shook his head. "I'm leaving tomorrow evening."

"Oh." There wasn't much I could do then. "Maybe we can go the next time you come to visit." I certainly couldn't bail on Cleo when she was the source of my future work.

"I'm afraid if we don't go now, we will lose our window of opportunity." Everything he said sounded as if he stole the phrasing from the BBC. "Perhaps you can call your employer and tell her you have an obligation." He said it as if he believed I did.

Even though I *wasn't* obliged to the man, I was curious. I pulled out my phone, dialed Cleo, and promised to work over for taking a few hours off tonight, even though my shifts really didn't work that way. If she noticed, she didn't mention it. I hung up and sucked in a shaky breath as I looked at Dominic. "Okay, but we should try to hurry."

"Splendid. Now, shall we go?" He offered his arm. Today, he was dressed in black slacks and a black shirt that made his pale skin look lighter, with a blood red tie. He could've been going off to a night at the office, or a club, even.

I didn't want to go, not really. Hunting sounded so savage when I didn't have to, not when I had a club and the ability to cover the marks and my tracks with a good glamour. Plus, the humans at the club knew about us and were trusted to keep all knowledge about vampires a secret. "I think I would prefer to go to the club. Hunting seems so barbaric."

There, I said it. I even lifted my chin a little, proud of myself.

Dominic looked at me without a trace of emotion on his face. He was a man of staunch expression. "Do I need to remind you that Jaxon was not supposed to turn you? Normally, I would be obligated to report his breech to the elders, but he's asked me not to. Right now, I'm inclined to go along with his request, but I would hate for anything to change that."

"Anything?" I didn't care for the implied threat.

He blinked slowly. "I need to make sure you can hunt without going rogue. Then I will be more comfortable keeping the information to myself."

"What does going rogue mean?" If I was going to end up rebelling, I should probably have known what it meant. Did he mean bloodlust? For all I know, his definition would be different from mine.

He shrugged. "It could be as simple as someone defying the rules or as severe as a vampire who has given in completely to his bloodlust, which jeopardizes our entire race."

He made it sound so clear-cut. But if there was one thing this vampire business had taught me, it was that nothing in the entire world was as straightforward as it looked.

But I nodded because he expected me to. I didn't need Jax to get in trouble.

He motioned for me to continue down the path. "We're going to venture out and find a house."

I didn't like the sound of this.

"Then I want you to gain entry so we can feed from the inhabitants."

"What?" I didn't know what I'd thought hunting was, but this wasn't it. Now that it was down to it, I really regretted not at least mentioning this to Jax. I assumed he knew, but what if he didn't? Dominic was his maker, after all. Butterflies plagued my stomach.

He sighed. "All the old tales about vampires being unable to enter a house without an invitation are true. Did you not know?"

"I don't often go into places I'm not invited." He had to be wrong. "You came into my house without me inviting you." Everything he said was suspect. His accent didn't make him sound trustworthy. Sexy, sure. But even an ogre sounded hot with a Scottish accent.

"You're a vampire. That changes the rules a bit." With his hand at the small of my back, he guided me to the car, then helped me inside before walking around to the driver side. When Jax did it, it was sexy and gentlemanly. When Dominic did it, it made me feel oppressed. Plus, I no more wanted to go hunting with Dominic than I wanted *anything* to do with him, but there I was in the car, buckled up and riding quietly beside him. He had a very persuasive personality.

He parked in a small subdivision on the other side of town. I was new to Chestnut Hill, and hadn't spent much time learning the neighborhoods, but this one was average. Split level houses with siding and brick, some landscaping, and a well-kept yard—but nothing like the shaped bushes and brick mansion we'd passed to get here.

"Off you go." What was I supposed to do?

When we walked from the street where he parked, up the sidewalk to the door of a nearby house, he moved to stand with his back against the wall, hiding as I knocked.

The door opened slightly, and a woman whose face was partially hidden by the door said, "Can I help you?"

"Hi. My car broke down and I was wondering if

you had a phone I could use? I fooled around and let mine die." I chuckled, but her eyes narrowed.

There were ten houses on this street. I didn't know why he'd picked this one, but the woman wasn't having it. She pulled an old flip phone out of her pocket and handed it to me. "Here."

"Oh...uh, thanks." Well, damn. That hadn't gone as planned. I dialed my home number, listened to the answering machine, and looked at the street signs as I pretended to speak to a tow company. When I "finished," I closed the phone and handed it back. "Thank you."

Dominic stage-whispered, "Use your compulsion."

I stepped forward and looked the woman in the eye, waited a second so she would get the idea, then spoke slowly and clearly, the way Jax had taught me. "You're going to let us in."

"Why would I do that?" The woman's brow creased as she stared at me. I'd not compelled her at all, and I had no idea why it didn't work. I glanced at Dominic and gave him a small shrug.

"You have to mean it. *Feel it.*"

She pulled back. "Who are you talking to?"

I looked at the woman and refocused my efforts. "You're going to let us in."

She blinked a couple times, and I had her. But then she shook her head before pushing the door. "I'm calling the police if you don't get in your car and get the hell out of here," she said as it closed.

If I was her, I would've called the cops already. But I focused again, harder, so hard, I thought I might fart. I pressed my palm to the door and kept it from closing all the way. "You're going to open this door and let us in."

This time, she nodded and swung the door open so Dominic and I could enter. "Very nice job."

I didn't even break wind.

She led us up a small flight of steps to her living room where her husband was seated watching football, a beer on a TV tray in front of him next to a half-eaten plate of fried chicken and mashed potatoes.

I maintained my focus on controlling the woman. "Sit down."

She did. This was the kind of wrong I didn't want to be, but I didn't have a choice. I sat beside her and fed while Dominic fed off the husband. I was careful not to drain her. Careful to heal her the way Jax had shown me.

We left without any fanfare or incident. Thank goodness. I just wasn't up for any drama. I felt like an ass feeding off of them in their own home as it was. When they felt fatigued and weak tomorrow, at least they wouldn't know why. I hoped not, anyway.

Dominic opened my car door. "Nicely done. Your restraint was magnificent."

If I was the kind of girl who needed praise, I would have enjoyed it. But I wasn't, and I didn't. Disgust bubbled inside of me at both of us and what he'd forced me to do when we had a club for this very purpose. It would take a pretty dire situation before I ever fed off a human in their own home ever again. From now on, my hunting would be limited to the club. Period.

# CHAPTER FIFTEEN

I went to work after my disgusting dinner with Dominic feeling dirty and angry at him, but more at myself for going along with it. I hadn't had a choice if it meant keeping Jax out of trouble. I had to prove I wasn't going to go rogue and embarrass or screw over the entire vampire race by bringing our presence into the light, so to speak.

I wrestled with guilt as I walked down the hall to Cleo's apartment. When I went in, she had her feet up on the coffee table. She spotted me and kicked them down, then winced. When I moved to help her, she held out her hand. "Too much, too soon. I keep forgetting to go slower."

But she had another stack of papers in hand. "I think you should go after the one on the top." When

I took the pages from her, she did a quick recap. "He's a puny little nudist who embezzled money from the clothing optional club he started. It's a fat bounty, and not a lot of strain involved."

Maybe this was how Jordan got so good. Going after the tiny skips until he earned the reputation for the big ones. I sure as hell would have complied if puny little Jordan showed up, and I'd heard he was the best of the best. I would also wonder what hidden talent he had that compensated for his size to make him the best. *Especially* after I heard his voice.

Cleo was right. Embezzling brought a high bounty fee because the bond was ridiculous.

I nodded. "I think this is our guy."

Stanley Kubnick, PCA.

While we waited for Kendra to show up—we didn't have any personal items this time, so she was going to have to use a location spell without it—I considered my image.

I needed a persona. A tag line. I pictured myself, handcuffing the skip, hauling him out of his apartment, turning to my imaginary cameraman, and saying, "I just took another bite out of crime," or something equally quippy and witty. Too bad I couldn't flash my fangs at the camera.

Of course, there was no camera and probably

never would be, and I certainly didn't want to get into the habit of flaunting my creature of the nightness, especially if I got so good at this that they gave me my own reality show.

Hey, a girl could dream.

When Kendra arrived, she laid out the spell ingredients, mixed them up, then closed her eyes. The Ouija board planchette she'd brought moved across the map to a spot across town near where I'd fed with Dominic.

"What do you think?" I looked at Cleo, then at Kendra. "Wanna try it?"

"He's a nudist who uses a computer to steal money. We can pick this guy up in our sleep." Kendra glanced at the photo again.

Cleo held up one finger. "I want to ride along this time. I haven't been out of the house except for hospitals in months, and I don't feel right taking a cut of the money just for sitting here reading files and faxes."

I hadn't discussed field trips with Tracy, but Cleo was a grown woman, and if she wanted to go on a skip trace with us, who was I to say no?

When I didn't answer right away, she huffed out a breath. "I can damn sure decide for myself if I sit in a car and watch you catch a perp."

She was right. She was an adult and she obviously knew the risks.

"Fine," I said. She pulled herself up and leaned on her walker. We moved a little slower because she had to take it easy, but what could it hurt to let her sit in the car?

"Shotgun." She moved a bit faster toward the elevator. "I want to be able to see out the windshield."

Kendra and I exchanged a grin. It was the least I could do. Besides, it would've been really hard for Cleo to maneuver into the back of the tiny vehicle.

When we got to the car, I climbed into the back seat. We had to get a bigger car. Maybe we should have taken mine. At least it was a four-door.

Once Cleo was in, Kendra drove her Prius to the neighborhood I'd just left with Dominic.

The sick feeling settled in my gut at the memory. I shook it because I didn't want to talk about it. Ever.

Kendra handed me the cuffs from her bag, and she pulled out the stun gun and a can of pepper spray. Cleo took the small spray can back. "Girl, you do not want to use this. It's hard to get a good aim, and the blowback could get you. Then it's a bitch to catch your skip." She put it back into Kendra's bag. "That stunner will do you fine."

Kendra nodded and squared her shoulders. "Let's do this."

As we walked up to the door of the colonial home, I glanced at the windows. There were lights on all over. "I think I want a catchphrase."

She glanced at me as we stuck to the shadows. "A catchphrase?"

"You know, like 'I'll be back!'" My Schwarzenegger impression left a bit to be desired, and she quirked a brow. "Or 'How you doin'?'" I had to speak her language.

Her eyes lit up. "Oh! Yeah! We totally need one of those."

"Right?"

I chuckled, and Kendra lowered her voice adding, "'If it weren't for you meddling kids' or 'Is that your final answer?'"

I nodded. "Both are valid."

She looked over her shoulder at me. "Let's do this."

I couldn't tell if we were mimicking catchphrases still or if she was ready. "Like really let's do this or is that another one?"

She rolled her eyes, shook her head, and looked at the house. "Let's go."

"Fine. I'm going." I headed closer to the house's

front door. "I thought maybe you were trying out a new one."

I shrugged, and then I heard it. A kamikaze yell. A scream and two feet landing on the ground.

Then, a blur of flesh so pale it made me look like *I* was tan streaked past me. Naked as the day he was born, Stanley Kubnick ran from the tree toward the house. He turned with a paintball gun locked and loaded. But I was faster than he could shoot, and his paintball sailed past me. It turned out, I wasn't faster than he could yell, though. "Aim and fire, Darlene!"

Luckily, Darlene's aim was bad, or I could've ended up skewered at the end of a wooden arrow. One foot higher than my left butt cheek, and I would've been a dead vampire. Instead, I had a hunter's arrow sticking out of my rump.

"Ow! You jerk!" I yelled at Stanley. Darlene was nowhere to be found.

He stood up and displayed his...goods. As impressive as they were, or rather, weren't, I wasn't here for his junk. "We're defending our home from invaders."

"You're trying your hand at hiding yourself from the long arm of the law, liar." I reached around to yank the arrow from my ass—thanking the heavens it was a blunt tip—then tossed it to the ground. "You're now also guilty of assaulting an officer of the bond agent who paid for you to be out of jail."

I didn't know if that was such a thing since I had crossed onto his property uninvited, but I made it sound official. "Now drop your weapon and call off Robin Hood."

When he made no move to comply, I pulled the paintball gun out of his hands and bent it in half. Hallelujah for superstrength.

When Darlene came down from the treehouse I hadn't even seen, Kendra aimed the taser at her. "Put it down, or you aren't going to like what happens." She had a spell she could've used—and I wouldn't have minded—to turn this chick into a toad, but I didn't know if she was threatening to use it or the taser. Either one would've made me happy. But honestly, my butt cheek had already started healing. It tingled.

Kendra nodded toward Darlene. "Slap the cuffs on him, and I'll keep this one back."

I yanked them from my waistband and smiled as I yanked his arms behind his back and clicked the bracelets around his wrists.

Darlene threw up her hands and stomped toward the porch. As she passed us, she spat toward Stanley. "Coward."

"Could you at least get me a pair of pants?" he asked weakly.

I agreed, and so did Kendra.

"Please. I don't want his junk on my car seats," Kendra said, and followed Darlene inside, soon returning with a pair of sweats we carefully slipped over Stanley's hips, trying to keep as much distance as possible.

Once he was no longer totally nude, off we went.

This was a big night for our team and as soon as Jordan saw us, he cocked a brow. "Well, well, well." He hugged Cleo, who insisted on coming inside with us. "Look at you, up and walking."

His hair stuck out in Einstein waves and curls, and his shirt—a Hawaiian luau print—was buttoned wrong. Cleo looked him up and down. "Who you got back there, Jordy?" She tried to peek around him but winced when she stretched to do it.

"Mind your beeswax, Missy. My social life is my business." He yanked the bond receipt from Kendra's hand. "Which one of you amateur sleuths am I writing this out to today?"

## CHAPTER SIXTEEN

By the time I returned home, it was so near dawn the sky was pink toward the east side, and I was exhausted from the dinner to the skip trace to dealing with Jordan and Kendra trying out every catchphrase she could think of. This was all new to me, and I still hadn't quite gotten used to being awake when the rest of the world slept.

I pulled into my driveway, and before I could open the door for myself, it was pulled open and Jax stood over me. His scowl was deep, and yet still extremely hot. I had a feeling my new catchphrase was going to end up being, "What did I do now?"

He huffed out a breath. "Why didn't you call me?"

"I didn't even know I was going to go. I mean,

he'd told me, but I guess I figured you were involved. Then when it came down to it, I didn't have time." Never had a truer truth been spoken. Not this day, at least. "He ambushed me as I was leaving for work."

I assumed he was talking about Dominic, because I already told him about working as a bounty hunter for the humans.

"Come on." He turned and walked across the street to his house. I gave the sky another quick glance, estimated I had about ten minutes for a butt-chewing, then I would need to be home, tucked in my bed.

I followed, slower, and he waited for me at the door. I walked past him toward the sofa. When he shut the door and turned, I held up my hand. "Hold on. If I'm going to get yelled at, I need to be comfortable. It's been a long night." I pushed the button for the reclining end.

He sighed. "I know how Dominic is, and I'm not going to yell at you." His voice was softer than I thought it would be, like a warm purr that vibrated through me. "But there are things I have to make sure you know."

I nodded because he'd come to sit on the coffee table in front of me. His cologne made me want to take a lot of deep breaths. "Like what?"

He sighed. "I broke a rule by making you, by biting you. It's punishable, should the elders decide not to justify your existence. To make a new vampire, there's a process and it's strictly monitored. There's paperwork and petitions and a census in the area has to be taken. Every new vampire has to be justified by the elders before they're made, then again after they're trained. Of course, there are exceptions, but they're rare and it takes a trial to clear the maker who creates a vampire without going through the proper channels."

It was all similar to what Paige had told me. But Paige had left out the part about Jax going to trial.

"Why? Wouldn't increasing the number give vampires strength? A position in society?" God, I hoped so. I didn't want to have to keep moving from town to town because everyone else aged, and I didn't, like in that vampire movie.

Jax shook his head. "The problem from before is that we were overpopulated. It made it too easy for the hunters, screwed with our food sources, and too many baby vampires went rogue. The elders live in fear of it happening again."

It all made sense, but I wasn't the one who made me. There had to be something he wasn't saying.

"Okay, but I'm already made. So, what can they really do?"

He sighed. Whatever he was about to say was not going to be pleasant. "If they decide I stepped out of bounds, I'll be punished with silver bonds for a while, or something equally as physically painful." That didn't sound fun. But he wasn't finished. "But they could rule that you'll have to be destroyed."

"Destroyed?" My voice squeaked as I said the word and sat straight up. No matter what it meant, it didn't sound good.

"Staked or decapitated." Okay. Yeah. Dead.

I nodded when his words registered. "What now?"

He sighed again. "That's why we have to be careful. The rules are strict."

"How often has the newly made vampire been destroyed?" Before I started to worry, maybe the number was low, something I could investigate as to the reasons the elders acted the way they did.

"I don't have statistics or anything..."

"Jax." He knew. There was no way he could deny it with all the guilt written on his face.

"I don't know of any who've been allowed to live."

Well, hell's fire. "Oh crap."

This was a situation that probably would have warranted a sturdier swear word, but I wasn't about to screw with karma, or the Big Guy, or whoever decided what action fate took in a situation.

I stared ahead at the ray of sunlight coming through the kitchen door. Jax followed my gaze and held out his hand. "Come on, you can stay here. All the bedrooms are light tight. You can have a spare."

If I was honest, I missed the sun...I missed being human, sleeping at night, and enjoying daylight, and even if I wasn't three sniffles into a good wallow, the chances of my brain shutting down enough so I could even doze, after I knew I was likely going to be *destroyed* soon, were slim.

This wasn't fair. I hadn't asked to be made a vampire. I hadn't planned to give up my life or my ability to get a suntan, but a group of vampires I'd never met before were going to decide whether or not to end me.

I slipped my hand into his and the old familiar tingles rushed up my arm and bloomed in my chest. At least I wouldn't die without knowing this kind of raw attraction to another person. Not that I hadn't been attracted before, but this was more...everything.

He stopped at a doorway. "Wait here a second."

He disappeared inside the room and came back a minute later with a t-shirt.

I should've gotten extra bonus points for not burying my nose in the fabric and inhaling it when he handed it to me. It smelled like him, so the restraint it took not to embarrass myself was an astounding amount.

At least, until he showed me to another room then walked out and shut the door behind him. Then I inhaled long and deep. Oh God. I was going to be wrapped in his scent while I slept in a bed in his house.

I crawled into bed, and was almost passed out when he knocked and poked his head in. I waved and he walked toward the bed, stood over me. "I came to tuck you in." After a second, he sat beside me, so his hip touched mine through the blanket. "I know you're probably worried, but I'm not going to let anything happen to you. I have a plan and will not let them take you."

I swallowed hard. "Because you're my maker?"

It took several seconds before he spoke. "No. That's not why." His smile was soft, as was the finger that brushed the hair off my forehead.

So badly, I wanted to ask why. I wanted to hear him say the words, but then he leaned in and pressed his soft, full lips against my cheek, and I couldn't have spoken if I tried. By the time I could speak again, he would probably have been asleep for a couple of hours. But I managed a smile.

"Sleep tight."

I was lying in this man's guestroom, wearing his shirt, wishing I was braver, brave enough to ask for a real goodnight kiss, but the moment was gone, and he was at the door, his finger on the light switch.

I waved. Because that was what I did when a beautiful man kissed me goodnight, even if it was only on the cheek.

## CHAPTER SEVENTEEN

When I woke, it was dusky outside, and I needed to get home, shower, and change before I went to work. I didn't necessarily mean to leave without saying goodbye, especially after our moment when Jax had tucked me in, but I didn't have a lot of choice since I didn't know where Jax was. Besides, I didn't want to look like I was snooping around his house.

When I walked outside, a long black stretch limo sat in the street and Jax and Dominic were climbing into the back. Paige stood at the edge of the yard watching, so I walked over to her. "What's going on?"

"Dominic is going home and he's taking Zara

with him." She crossed her arms and watched them leave.

I nodded because I was glad to see Dominic go. After what Jax had explained, with Dominic gone, I would be able to breathe again. For a little while anyway.

Instead of sticking around with Paige, I walked across the street to my house. There would be time later to talk to Jax about everything he'd told me and to thank him for letting me stay at his place.

When I checked my voicemails on my phone, I saw that Cleo had called and said she didn't really need me to come in if I wanted to stay home. That sounded great to me. Two skips in as many days and all this news from Jax had put my mind into a whirl-wind. No way was I turning down a night I could use to decompress.

My fridge was nothing more than a magnetic bulletin board now, and Luke had made sure to attach cards for each of the openings at his gallery. There was one he'd been bugging me to come to. A new artist I was "just going to fall in love with." I doubted it since my taste in art wasn't nearly as sophisticated as his, but it would be nice to get dressed up and be among people.

I called Paige and invited her, and Ransom, then

called Kendra. "Gallery opening tonight. Want to go?" I didn't even bother with a hello when she answered. These days, we were way past pleasantries.

"Formal or casual?"

"You know Luke. Everything he does is formal. He's probably wearing something from the Liberace library, and we'll be expected to sparkle to match." I loved Luke's style, but he outshone the art almost every single time.

"Give me thirty minutes."

"Excellent." I took those same minutes to shower, and blow dry my hair, then to exfoliate and shine. Whatever anyone said, becoming a vampire was good for the skin. Mine had never been clearer nor my pores smaller.

As a group, we were elegance personified. Kendra and I had on our little black dresses. Mine had gold roses embroidered across the low neckline. It fell off the shoulders and had three quarter sleeves. The body of the dress hugged my curves and stopped just above my knees. I'd worn my black, strappy heels.

Kendra's black dress was accented with lace and a long flowing skirt that fell to about mid-calf. She wore a sexy pair of stilettos.

Paige had on a sleek navy-blue pantsuit with a red cami under her jacket, and heels that matched.

Ransom had opted for a suit that I guessed was designer and cost more than the last bounty I collected. Maybe. Did suits cost that much?

Ransom had arranged for a limousine, which seemed to be one of his feature functions today, and we piled into the opulent ride. He'd also arranged for tulip glasses of "wine"—blood laced with wine, actually—and the flavor of the grapes didn't make me want to vomit, so I drank and smiled while Kendra drank a glass of unlaced Chardonnay.

We arrived in style, and since it had been a while since I'd had anything more flavorful than AB negative, I was a bit tipsy, but not sloppy. Just happy. Happy to be among friends and seeing my brother's place in all its glory.

Luke, ever the social butterfly, flitted from guest to guest and when he came to me, he threw his arms out and wrapped me in a hug. The abrupt ending of said hug sent me shoulder first into a wall so Lukey-poo could fawn over Ransom. Ransom's cheeks flushed with color. I didn't know if I was imagining it because a lot of people reacted to Luke this way or if it was real, but I nudged Paige. "I love when his cheeks do that."

She nodded. "Kind of makes him a real person, which I sometimes seriously doubt."

We chuckled and Kendra eyed up the bartender, then hid her face behind her hands. "Oh God. It's Xander."

Even I remembered Xander. He was an ex who'd cheated on her with another witch from a coven she'd been scoping out. Needless to say, she hadn't joined that coven.

"I didn't know he was a bartender." I couldn't remember what his occupation was, but surely I would've remembered it being bartending.

"Yeah." She rolled her eyes and turned away so if he looked our way, he would see a lot of shoulder, a few inches of spine, and her hairdo.

There was another bar on the opposite side of the gallery. "I'm going over there."

She linked arms with Paige and off they went while I stared at a deep blue painting. It looked like broad strokes of blue paint spread unevenly over a canvas. I didn't get it.

"Hello."

I looked left then right. I didn't see anyone, so I moved to the next painting because a crowd had formed around "Blue."

As I stepped in front of the next painting—multicolored splashes I couldn't make sense of—the masculine "hello" voice said, "I love the way the artist used red to show anger in the skyline of the city."

Oh! A city! "I didn't recognize that it was a city."

We chuckled together, and he used his finger to point out the lines of the building. But I'd moved on from the painting to the man. He was gorgeous. If Jax was Brad Pitt, this guy was George Clooney. Curly black hair, gray eyes, a body designed to be worshipped. He was scrumptious.

As soon as I had the thought, my heart raced— my body still reacted despite my back-from-the-dead lack of heartbeat—then guilt powered through me. I'd had a moment with Jax. Here I was drooling over this guy. But, oh my. There was a lot to drool over.

Not to the exclusion of his voice, either. "I'm Blake." He held out his hand and squeezed mine softly. More heart pounding action ensued, and I was there for it.

"I'm Hailey. Nice to meet you."

"So nice to meet a fellow art connoisseur." Now he was poking fun, but I could roll with it. "Want to know the truth?"

I nodded. He could've quoted me a line from the Pennsylvania State Constitution, and I would've stayed right there and listened to the richness of his tone and soft cadence with which he spoke.

"I've been waiting to talk to you since you came in, but I couldn't figure out how to strike up a conversation about a plain blue canvas." He was a northerner, but not New England-ish or New York or anywhere I could've placed him by the slight accent. I was normally so good at accents.

I couldn't concentrate wholly on the words, or I might've embarrassed myself with a swoon, and in these heels, I could've broken a bone. While healing might've happened with the swift speed of a vampire, the initial fall would've caused a scene. Besides, being a vampire didn't remove pain.

"Really?" I could just see his fangs when he smiled and paid careful attention to the pale skin. "Are you a"—I lowered my voice to a whisper—"vampire?" He nodded and wagged his eyebrows.

"Do you know Jaxon Parsons?" I asked.

He smiled. "Yes. We've met." His gaze burned up my body.

I turned for a second to see where Paige and Kendra had gone. It could only up my cool quotient for them to see me standing with this guy, plus the intensity of his attention was a bit overwhelming.

They were coming my way. Close. I turned back

to Blake, but he was gone. I scanned the crowd. Standing on my tiptoes, I looked for the deep black of his hair. His height was easily taller than most of the folks in the room. But it wasn't like he'd just found me boring and walked on. This guy had *vanished*.

It took almost an hour of pretending to like the paintings with Paige and Kendra before they moved on while I stared at a pumpkin landscape—a field of actual pumpkins.

"You know, you shouldn't stand so close to the paintings. You make them seem dull and without life."

I turned again, and there he was. Blake. This time, I was the one flushing with color. It was a line, but it was a good one, and no matter how hard I tried not to be, I was the kind of girl who fell for all the good lines.

I breathed out because I didn't want to tell him that underneath the makeup and updo, the sparkly dress and four-inch heels, I was a normal, rather plain woman, but not telling him seemed deceitful. I had enough strikes in my naughty column.

"I don't usually dress quite so...fancy." I motioned toward my dress.

"Good." He pulled his bowtie and it hung loose,

the black making his crisp white shirt all the more stark and pristine. "Me, either." He grinned. "Would you like to get out of here and go get a drink?"

It had been a *super* long time since anyone had asked me for drinks. But it felt disloyal to Jax. What did it say about me that I could go from lusting after one man to immediately lusting after another? "I really should stay. It's my brother's gallery." The lie rolled easily off my tongue. It *was* Luke's gallery, but that wasn't why I didn't want to go.

Speaking of which, Luke laid his hand on my back. "Little sister. Who is your new friend?"

"Blake, this is my brother Luke, the owner of this beautiful establishment. Luke, this is Blake." Had I really not caught his last name?

"It's a pleasure to meet you," Blake said. His voice was more smooth than maple syrup stirred with melted butter as he shook Luke's hand. "This is a stunning exhibit."

Blake winked at me, and I wasn't sure if he was talking about the artwork or me. The words said one thing, but the look said something else. My heart skipped and stuttered. The effect this man had on the muscle memory of the human I'd been was almost as potent as my reaction to Jax.

Luke cocked his head at me and widened his

eyes out of Blake's view, then smiled when I turned back to include Blake in whatever conversation I managed to have around my awkwardness.

From the corner of my eye, I caught sight of Paige and Ransom coming our way. As I was about to mention to Blake that he was going to be quite popular with my friends, he was gone. Again. This guy was some kind of vampire escape artist.

For the rest of the evening, we puttered around the gallery, staying until most other people were gone.

As we waited for the limousine to pick us up, I felt his eyes on me, and I turned to give a little wave.

Paige nudged me. "Who are you waving at?" She craned her neck in the direction where Blake had been standing, and again, he was gone.

I chuffed out a breath, frustrated. The one time a really hot guy paid attention to me, and I couldn't show him off because he kept disappearing. "I met a guy named Blake, a vampire. Although I'm starting to wonder if he's real or a figment of my imagination."

Maybe I even imagined Luke meeting him. Wouldn't have surprised me considering all the new things going on in my life. A bout of crazy hallucinations that made me a sex object wasn't as out of line as I hoped it would be.

Why was no one applauding that I'd met a man? Paige looked around with interest, her face a little puzzled. "I don't know a Blake," she murmured.

Ransom walked beside me. "Hey, I'll meet you guys back at Jax's house."

There wasn't further explanation, but there were red cheeks and a slight pep to his step as he turned and headed back to where Luke was standing, beaming at him.

I sat in the limo while Paige and Kendra gossiped over the clothes they'd seen, hairstyles, men. I thought of Blake, those eyes, that deep black hair. It wasn't every day a man looked at me and spoke such flirty words. Not that I needed the validation. I was happy in sweats and jeans and didn't care much if anyone liked the way I looked. But there was something about a man in a tuxedo comparing me to art and me winning that made my heart pitter patter. It had been a good night.

## CHAPTER EIGHTEEN

I side-stepped a jab. "Heard you went to the gallery opening the other night." Jax's voice sounded casual, but something was off. He didn't miss a lot of footwork, and he stumbled like he'd misjudged a third foot.

"Yeah."

"I heard you met a vampire." His voice went hard, and this jab was designed to maim, but easy to redirect. "Blake." He fourteen-year-old-girl mimicked.

"Wow. Are you jealous?" There was a new flutter in my belly, and it had Jax's jealousy written all over it.

He scoffed. "No. Of course not. This is my territory and if a new vamp is in town, he needs to let me know."

"You keep a register book?" I asked.

He shot me a bit of side-eye that meant he didn't appreciate my question. I got it a lot with him, so it was easy to recognize these days. "No, wise guy, but since the population of vampires in any area is monitored, I need to know when mine changes."

Made sense.

"Any vampire who isn't an *infant*"—he threw that word around sometimes when I did something he didn't like—"knows to give me a courtesy heads up."

"Oh. Sorry." Probably not as much as I should've been, but I wasn't completely buying his story either.

"That's enough for today." He jerked off his boxing gloves and stuffed them into the equipment bag in the corner of his basement then stalked toward the stairs. "I'm going to hit the shower."

There was no invitation involved, so I stowed my stuff in the locker he'd assigned to me, then I went home. Would've been nice to have a shower with Jax, but whatever.

I didn't remember whether or not I locked the door, because sometimes when I headed over to train with Jax or Ransom or both, I left it open. But I never left it unlatched, able to be pushed without turning the knob.

When I walked inside, I knew. Someone had been in my house and might've still been there. The unlatched door was my first clue, the second was my living room looked like a tornado had gone through it. I picked up the glass bowl where I normally tossed the keys with the intent to use it as a weapon. It was heavy and could do some serious damage.

After a minute, I walked out onto the porch because there was nothing in my place that hadn't been touched, rifled through, disturbed, and set askew. I dialed Jax's number and told him what had happened. I couldn't call the cops because I didn't know what or who was in my house. Or who could still be there. It'd be terrible for a cop to die because he came upon a vampire in my home.

What the hell? This was nuts.

I stood near the steps and waited, still holding the crystal bowl and ready to strike and didn't relax until Jax appeared on the steps.

"Wait here," he growled. Whoa. Jax did *not* like my house being ransacked.

Whatever. Didn't mean I was doing as he said. I was freaked out, but I was still bad to the bone.

I followed him inside and bumped into his back

when I gasped at the streams of shaving cream on my bathroom floor. After I bumped into him, and he stepped a foot into the mess, he turned and narrowed his eyes at me. But I continued to stare at the floor. "That's just rude," I whispered.

"I told you to stay outside." He tried to intimidate me with his glower, but it didn't work.

I shrugged.

"You can't stay here. You shouldn't be in here at all." He arched one handsome eyebrow.

"I live here." This was my sofa and my table. My clothes were in the bedroom.

"You can stay at my place." He moved out of the doorway and stepped backwards into me this time. "Okay, this isn't going to work."

"I could walk in front of you?" Anything to be helpful.

He glared, and I took a step back.

"Listen, Hailey, I can't get a sense of anyone. That means it's either a witch or a very old vampire." If troubled had a look, Jax was wearing it—narrowed eyes, tight mouth, ticking jaw. "If you won't stay with me, let me send Paige to stay with you. Train every night whether you have to go to work or not." He wasn't playing. This was serious. "Let her stay until we figure out who was here."

I nodded; I didn't have another choice. Plus, I would sleep better if someone else was here. If that someone was also a vampire, especially a bad ass like Paige, sleep wouldn't be a problem.

Since it was still early enough after we cleaned up the mess in my house, Paige and I went online, and I showed her how to look up the skip traces. Cleo had given me a password into Jordan's system, so I could keep track in case I wanted to work on days I didn't have a shift at her place.

"Ooh. Look at this one." I didn't often check the crimes, I just looked at the bounty receipt fees. This one was huge.

"He's a murderer." That incited a smile as wide as I'd ever seen on a person, human or otherwise.

I dialed Jordan. When he answered with a "Hidey-ho!" I started in.

"I want Aaron Hightower."

He clucked his tongue. "No way. You can't handle Hightower."

He was almost six inches taller than I was. Shamefully, he was about twenty-five pounds lighter. I hadn't gone after a skip yet I hadn't brought in.

"I can handle Hightower. I'm a Bond Girl." Just that quick and easy, our new enterprise had a name. "I am one third of Bond Girls Recovery." It could have been a twelve-step program or a skip trace agency.

"I think 007 might have a problem with that," Jordan drawled.

"Let him sue me. Now can I have Hightower or not?" This was serious money. Big cash.

"You're quite the steel magnolia, aren't you?" he drawled, then sighed. "I suppose, but if he eats you up and spits you out, don't come crying to me." He hung up before I could answer and that was okay. My reply probably would've changed his mind.

"Bond Girls?" Paige chuckled. "I'm not wearing a bikini top with my leather pants."

"An ejection seat would be cool, though. Life changing if we're honest." I smiled and called Kendra. When she answered the phone, I sing-songed, "We've got one."

It was all I had to say to get the reaction I wanted. "I'm on my way."

She hung up, and Paige and I waited the ten minutes it took her to arrive. Five more for her to get us a location with her spell and about thirty more to drive to within a few blocks from where we'd found Zara. I didn't believe in coincidence, but this was a little close for me. A bit easy.

I had a job to do, though. Money to collect when we finished. I glanced at Paige. "You mind watching the back?"

We were at an apartment building right beside a coffee shop. How I would've loved a place like that back in the day.

She nodded. "Yup." Kendra went to hand her the taser and Paige smirked. "I think I'm okay without it. You keep it."

In Kendra's defense, I'd taken the taser once and I had the same superpowers Paige did.

I filled Kendra in on the Bond Girl situation, and she smiled. "Heck, yeah. I'll be a Bond Girl."

As I rounded the corner to take my position at the front of the building, Blake walked out of the coffee shop, a cup marked K-Macchiato in one hand, a newspaper in the other. He stopped short and it was good the cup had a lid, or I would've been covered in scalding and aromatic coffee.

"Hey, Hailey." He tucked the paper under the arm with the coffee and slid his now free hand down my arm. "How are you?" He spoke slowly with his brow wrinkled, as if he was surprised, or like he thought maybe I was stalking him.

"I'm doing great. How are you?" He eyed Kendra

while I spoke, then focused on me again, and my skin warmed under his gaze. "This is my friend Kendra."

He smiled and gave her a slight nod, then looked at me again. There was something about this guy that spoke to mystery and intrigue and such beauty I could hardly breathe. For a second, I wondered if he knew how pleasing he was to look at. Then I wondered where such silly thoughts came from. They certainly couldn't be mine since every other minute of the day, I was busy thinking of Jax.

"I'm so glad I ran into you." I'd run into him, but whatever. "Would you want to go to dinner with me tomorrow night?"

I was a vamp. He was, too. I didn't like hunting for my dinner. What did he mean by going to dinner?

Kendra nudged me. "Hails, we need to go. Business?"

She was right. I glanced at Blake. There was nothing to do but let him down gently, so he didn't kill me in the street. Men like him probably didn't get a lot of rejections, and I needed to be prepared in case he took it badly. I braced myself. "I can't."

Not because of Jax, but because I preferred to dine at the club. It was easier and way less savage.

Not that I wanted to explain it to such a suave and sophisticated vampire.

"Another time, then." He leaned in and kissed my cheek then pulled back, winked, and smiled. Then he walked away like he hadn't just set my world upside down.

"Holy hot guy, Batman. Who the heck was that?" Kendra's mouth gaped open as I opened the door to the apartment building and walked inside to the stairwell.

"I met him at Luke's gallery. He must live around here or something."

"Well, aren't you just a man-magnet these days?" She shook her hands out.

I hadn't even told her about Jax tucking me in the other night. I shook my head. I had no idea what was going on. Maybe being a vampire had made me more attractive, or maybe I was attractive to vampires because there was a rule or a law or some elder edict that said they couldn't date human women. Or maybe there was a shortage of vamp women. I didn't know, but neither was I going to shun the admirers who'd chosen *me* to admire.

I walked to the second-floor apartment and knocked on the door. "Aaron Hightower?" He was in his thirties, accused of killing his wife; his uptown, socialite, society pages wife. He'd pleaded not guilty according to his bond report. I couldn't believe they'd let him out on bail. Of course, a guy who killed his wife uptown where the mansions were on acreage the size of Chestnut Hill got treated a little differently from guys who killed their wives in the projects downtown.

Furniture scraped against the floor inside the apartment. This guy wasn't putting it in front of the door so he could let us in. Kendra stepped back and made room for me.

I pushed the door open like it wasn't made of more than a few feathers and found Hightower trying to make a run out of the window to the fire escape. Before I made it all the way into the room, he jumped, and I ran to the window and looked down. Paige had him on the ground and was hog-tying him with a cord she'd brought with her, which looked suspiciously like the nylon cord I used to hold my curtains open.

Whatever, it was fine. She had him. As fast as we could, Kendra pulled the car into the alley so we could load him in and take him to the precinct for our receipt.

"Bond Girls ride again!" Kendra fist pumped the air, and I smiled. This was a brilliant partnership. We were going to succeed all the way to the bank.

By the time we went back to Jordan, roused him from his sleep and collected the payout, it was almost dawn again. He was suitably impressed. "I might have to start throwing some real action your way," he said as he signed the check.

I dragged myself home, and again found Jax outside waiting for me. "You cut dawn close," he said. But he smiled.

"What are you doing here?" I'd been very into my skip tracing.

He lifted his hand as if to touch my arm, but let it fall again. "I thought maybe you should stay at my place."

Not this again.

"What about Paige?" Her staying at my place had worked out pretty well. Not as well as me staying at his since *that* night I got a kiss. Chaste as it was, it counted in my book since it was the only one I'd had in months.

"She'll stay there, too." His place was huge with so many rooms, we wouldn't have ever run into each other had he not put me into a room close to his. "But I need you to be safe." He cocked his head. "I watched your house all night to make sure no one went in or out, but I don't want to take the chance of them coming while we're sleeping."

It made sense, but I couldn't stay at his place indefinitely. Much as I might've wanted to.

With a sigh, I relented. At least for now. "All right." I walked across the street with him just as the first rays of daylight streaked across the morning sky.

## CHAPTER NINETEEN

Since I didn't have to work tonight for Cleo, I planned to sleep in, but the phone's shrill ring had other ideas, or at least the person responsible for the ringtone had other ideas.

I answered even though I didn't know the number. "Hello?"

Smooth baritone floated over the phone line. "Good evening, Hailey. I was hoping you would be free to join me for dinner this evening."

I knew the voice, recognized it as belonging to Blake immediately. As flattering as his invitation, I couldn't go to dinner with him when I'd just woken up at Jax's house.

But more important, he was giving off a vibe,

even over the phone. "How did you get this number?" I asked.

I remembered our every interaction vividly and at no point had I provided my number. If Luke had given it to him, we were going to have yet another boundaries talk.

Blake chuckled, and even down the line, it sounded hollow. It hadn't sounded like that when we met the first time, I would've noticed. I was almost sure anyway. "I have money, and money gives me choices, opportunities, and options." I wondered which of the three categories I fell into. His answer told me nothing.

But I moved on. "I appreciate the offer, but I'm involved with someone."

Kind of. Close enough, anyway. I was sleeping in another man's house. The fact didn't escape me because the whole place was scented with Jax's cologne. His room was across the hall from mine.

I wasn't sure what exactly we were, but I wanted us to be more. We definitely had the chemistry for it. The tingles. The delicious magic that made my body behave like it was still human when he touched me, or gazed at me, or when we trained. When he wrapped his body around mine, I could feel every muscle and rippling valley as it touched mine.

If only he would stop pulling back when we got close.

Thinking of the devil, he knocked softly and poked his head in the door. I held up one finger. "Thank you for the offer, but I have to go."

I didn't wait for a goodbye or even a reply before I hung up.

Jax smiled and walked fully into the room. "Everything okay?"

I nodded and took a second to take him in. This guy had a way of wearing jeans that made me grateful for denim. He had eyes like a chameleon. Yesterday, I'd been sure they were hazel. Today, they were more turquoise that matched his shirt. His hair had that perfect mixture of tousled and textured that made it look like he'd just raked his fingers through it. There was nothing not to like.

"Yeah," I said. "It was Blake."

His voice changed—gentle to gruff—and his eyes narrowed. "Blake the vampire?"

I nodded. "He asked me to dinner."

Calling it dinner rather than hunting sounded deceitful to me, but I let it go for now. I wasn't going to change an entire race's verbiage, nor did I care to try. But it annoyed me anyway.

Jax shook his head and scoffed. "Presumptuous

bastard."

I hid a smile by pulling my lips between my teeth until it went away on its own. I couldn't stop the question though because I wanted an answer. "Are you jealous?"

"No." He didn't even blink when he said it, but he didn't look directly at me either. "Jealous." He rolled his eyes. "Whatever."

I nodded and didn't tell him he had all the classic signs. "What's the problem then?"

He narrowed his eyes again, staring at me hard for a couple of seconds, then shook his head again. "I'm the guy he needs to register with. Everyone in this city and the surrounding area knows it and would tell him."

Oops. Was I supposed to have told him? "He still hasn't?" It was obvious, but sometimes I needed to hear my own voice to remind me not to stay locked in my own head. Plus, I didn't want Jax to realize I'd missed an opportunity to tell Blake he needed to see Jax.

Wait, but I did ask him. At the gallery. "I asked him if he knew you, and he said you've met. So, I assumed he had."

Jax shook his head. "No. He has not. I don't know any vampire named Blake."

That was odd. Had this guy given me a false name?

"That's why you're angry?" I wanted to hear him say it. More, I wanted him to tell me he was jealous, but I mostly just liked his voice, whether he was angry or happy or joking or bossy. Maybe I wanted him to deny being jealous, because his protests and denials spoke the truth his words did not.

"Yeah." Again, he didn't look at me. "Absolutely." A second later, "It's a matter of respect."

"Respect. Right." But my cold, dead little heart leaped because he was lying, and there was no denying it.

He sighed and shook his head, then glanced up at me and waited a second before he spoke. When he did, his voice was softer. "Do you want to go to the club?"

I imagined his invitation as a date more than my maker taking care of my nutritional needs. I nodded.

He motioned to a small piece of my luggage sitting inside the door. "I had Paige go to your place and get you some clothes and some of your personal stuff." He shrugged and put his hands in his pockets. "I wanted you to be comfortable."

It was thoughtful. His kindness was sexy. I couldn't help but tease him. "As my maker?"

His head bobbed up. But he said, "No."

He backed out of the room before I could ask any further questions, and I snuggled under the cover for a few seconds, letting the fact that he'd considered my comfort wash over me. I wondered what he'd been like before he was a vampire. Who he'd been in that life. I wanted to know more. So much more.

THE CLUB WAS HOPPING. For a Wednesday in the first week of April, the place was crowded with gyrating bodies and intoxicated humans. I glanced at the crowd, scoping out my dinner, and I recognized the black hair, and the smile when it aimed itself at me coupled with a wink. I elbowed Jax, making the mistake of taking my eyes off Blake. "He's here."

"Who?" he asked absently.

"Blake." If only I could get his attention so easily when I hadn't messed up at training or when I was just being my normal self.

His head snapped toward the dance floor. "Where?"

I looked back again and pointed, but Blake was gone. Again. "This guy..." If he wasn't a descendant of Houdini, someone had messed up the family tree.

But more, what was Blake doing here?

"Stay here." He waved Paige over and she stood beside me. It was a little embarrassing, but I didn't protest.

I waited quietly, watching Jax as he moved through the crowd, as he circled the floor, as more vampires came out—where they'd come from, I had no idea—and blocked exits, checked the clientele, and watched Jax for cues.

Jax came back a moment later. "He's gone." He swore the big one and slammed his hand against the bar top. The sound reverberated along the wood counter.

I nodded because all my heebie-jeebies had gone away.

"Did you tell him where you were going?" Jax stared into my eyes, trying to compel an answer.

It didn't work. "No. I didn't. You didn't ask me to come here until after I hung up."

He nodded at the bartender, then handed me a glass of blood. "Drink up. We're out of here."

I sighed—the dreamy kind—because he shielded my body from view as I drank which put him very close to me. So close that if he had body heat, I would've felt it. I was never going to complain about that.

# CHAPTER TWENTY

I n the car, he informed me, like I had no choice in the matter, "You're coming home with me."

I wasn't arguing because seeing Blake there, smiling at me, then his smarmy wink, had freaked me out enough I didn't want to be alone. There was something off. I could feel it.

I shivered, and Jax slid his hand over mine as he drove. He'd left Paige at the club with Ransom to talk to anyone who might've seen or spoken to Blake. The windows of Jax's car were blacked out with tint, and it was almost midnight on a night with no moon. If not for the dashboard lights, I wouldn't have been able to see at all.

"Thank you for everything." It felt inadequate, but if I started pouring my heart out right now, there was a chance it would never end, and I couldn't risk it.

He gave my hand a squeeze and when he pulled to a stop light, looked at me. "It's my pleasure to take care of you."

The words were hot syrup, and I was pancakes. It made sense. Syrup was tree blood, and now I loved blood. Something inside of me clicked. "Your pleasure?"

"Mmm." Oh, heavenly hotness. That sound settled in my belly and spread heat—the fiery kind—through me. "My pleasure." This time, when he spoke, his voice was low and deep, so darn sexy I imagined his breath against my skin as he spoke, his hands caressing, mouth tasting.

*My* pleasure.

I wasn't worldly or sophisticated enough with men to know how to react, but I hoped he couldn't read my mind. Well, all but a very tiny sliver of my consciousness hoped he couldn't. The little part of me who hoped he could, who wouldn't have minded him knowing what I wanted so I didn't have to ask for it out loud and risk his rejection.

He pulled the car into his garage and shut off the engine. We sat for a second, neither of us looking at the other, his fingers still threaded through mine. "We should go in."

I nodded, unable to form words, because the huskiness of his voice along with the naughty thoughts in my head had me imagining all kinds of new experiences. I'd never made out with a man in a car. Not even when I was a teenager, and I was expected to do things like that.

We weren't inside for more than a few seconds when the doorbell chimed, and I glanced at Jax. His shoulders tensed. Paige and Ransom lived there with him, so they didn't knock, and he didn't receive a lot of other visitors in the middle of the night. Vamps who wanted to see him often met him at the club. Or called to schedule a meeting.

He walked to the door and swung it open. Blake stood in the doorway. "Miss Whitfield." He nodded to me as he walked past Jax. When he winked again, that same freaky feeling crept over my skin.

Jax shut the door and turned to watch Blake as he sat on the sofa. I probably shouldn't have stood there gaping, but I didn't have anywhere else to go.

"Blake Winslow, Mr. Parsons." He glanced at Jax then held out a hand Jax took and probably tried to squeeze until the bones crushed. When he let go, he stepped back, and Blake smiled again. "I went to your club tonight to meet you, but I didn't want to interrupt your evening."

"Yet here you are." Jax was more ungracious, harder than I thought the situation demanded, but I wasn't a centuries old vampire who was in charge of all the other vampires in the area. Maybe this was his way of asserting his power. Who was I to judge?

Blake smiled. "Yes. Here I am." He added, "Finally." His voice dropped and he lowered his head as if he was trying—and failing—to sound chagrined that he hadn't arrived sooner.

Jax clenched his jaw. "I have to wonder why the delay if you knew where to find me the entire time."

The back door opened, and Paige and Ransom walked into the living room from the kitchen. Blake and Jax were locked in a stare-off that Jax won, because Blake blinked and smiled, then chuckled.

"I'm ashamed to admit, but I suppose I need to make this right." Suddenly, he was pouring on the slow southern charm. I hadn't noticed even the hint of an accent before, then a slightly Yankee one, but now he was giving Miss Scarlett a run for her money. "As much as it pains me to admit it, I was a coward. Intimidated by the legend of Jaxon Parsons. Your lore is widespread and well-known among our kind."

I might've bought the intimidation line had he

not sounded like he was about to clutch his pearls and shout that Atlanta was burning. Jax was intimidating in ways not all men were or could ever be. He had power in every pore of his body. What a body!

Jax turned away and rolled his eyes at me, then walked toward a credenza in the corner of the room away from the sofa where Blake had perched. "What brings you to Chestnut Hill? To Pennsylvania at all?" He opened a drawer and pulled out a ledger book, then flipped to the back and pulled a pen from the desk.

"Visiting friends." He glanced at me and smiled again. "Met a pretty girl. Thought I would try my luck."

I wasn't a prize to be awarded to the lucky winner. Though his words were the kind designed to make a girl swoon, I wasn't swooning. I looked away from his smile, from the wink I suspected was coming. How had I found him charming at first?

Jax shot me a look, then glanced back at Blake. "How long will you be staying?"

"I don't have a set itinerary, but I'm thinking a week, maybe two." He looked me up and down again. "There are various factors involved in my decision."

"Various factors?" Jax cocked one eyebrow, and a growl rumbled low in his chest.

Blake grinned. "I should let you get back to your evening."

But when he stood to leave, he walked toward me, took my hand in his and brought it to his mouth to press a kiss against my knuckles. I pulled back and wiped my hand on the fabric of my skirt against the side of my thigh. Then he was gone. A ruffle of curtains and papers in his wake.

"He just showed up here?" Ransom scowled as he passed me to close the still open door.

It bothered me, too, that Blake seemed to have access to a lot of information I wasn't sure he would've been able to come by easily. My address and phone number, for example. Although, since it was expected that he registered with Jax, maybe coming into a new place supplied him with the subliminal information he needed. I still wasn't sure how all this vampire mumbo-jumbo worked. Yet. I seemed to be learning on the slow curve.

"Like he owned the place." Jax might've been exaggerating, but not by a lot.

Blake had breezed in, sat before us like he was invited, and had spoken like he was the man in charge, though his words were sufficiently deprecating.

"You buy that whole *you intimidate me* crap?" I wasn't sure if Paige was asking me or Jax, so I stayed quiet.

Jax shrugged. "It's lame if it's true."

"Yeah. Something's off." Ransom crossed his arms and his chest looked broader, thicker than I noticed before. "Maybe he's about to go rogue?"

Jax nodded and puffed out a breath. "Maybe."

I edged toward the door. I needed a night away from Jax. A minute to clear my head and catch my breath because I was in danger of falling hard for all his manly-man vibes and uber-protective-ness. While I could and would take care of myself, it was intoxicating to have someone who *wanted* to take care of me. Until I knew for sure he wasn't this way only because I was his 'infant vampire,' I wasn't letting myself risk falling any harder or crushing any more than I already was.

"Where are you going?" He stopped me as I reached for the knob.

I dropped my hand and turned. "I thought I would spend the night at home."

"Why?"

No way was I coming forth with *that* truth.

"I, um, I-I-I planned a sleepover with my girls and Luke." I glanced at Paige hoping she would jump in and save my horribly executed lie. When she didn't, I smiled at her, probably looking like I was trying to pass a kidney stone. "Right, Paige?"

It took her a second after Jax looked at her. "Right! Yeah. A sleepover." She nodded a bit more enthusiastically than the situation required. But neither Jax nor Ransom stopped us when we went outside and across the street.

When I got inside my house, I decided to make my fib a truth and called Kendra and Luke. For one night, I'd had enough of being a vampire and enough of being a Bond Girl. I wanted to be normal, with friends around me who could make me laugh and for a few minutes forget the crazy twists and turns my life had taken over the last few months. If I could get one normal night, all the others wouldn't have been so shocking. I hoped anyway.

Paige and I would be sufficient to protect us while Jax worked on who Blake was and why he was here. That would do for now.

Luke arrived in furry slippers and pajamas with fur, a Chanel bag full of snacks over his arm, and wine for them and a few packets of blood for me and Paige. Kendra came a few minutes later, and we spread pillows and blankets on the floor in front of the TV.

Conversation flowed, and even Paige told stories about her vampy ex. "My last one was pathetic and hated the fact that I worked with Jax. At first, I thought he was jealous of Jax. Then he applied to be one of Jax's enforcers."

"Really?" I frowned, and knew at that moment I would never understand men. It didn't matter what species they were.

Paige nodded. "Yeah, but when Jax made it clear that he'd have to take orders from me, the jerk pitched a fit. So, I threw him out on his ass."

Kendra raised her glass in the air. "Good riddance!"

Paige clinked her glass with Kendra's. "That's what I said. He wasn't my true mate anyway. Just someone to pass the time with."

"True mate?" I asked, not hearing that term mentioned among the vamps.

"Yeah. Every vampire has a mate. The one destined to be their perfect match and to spend their very long and lonely existence with."

I fell silent and sipped my wine laced blood to hide my reaction. At least I hoped it did. Jax had a mate out there somewhere. That meant I could never fall for him because he would leave me like the other men in my life did.

This was why I was resolved not to get into another serious relationship ever again.

Luke, the talker, the highlight of every party, changed the subject. I was glad. "Oh, ladies. You have no idea what it's like to be a mere mortal man."

I chuckled. "Do tell."

"Well, I'm dating a vampire. I work all day because...hello. I'm human and that's when the gallery's open. Then, I play all night."

Paige chuckled like she had information the rest of us didn't. "Ransom can play all night long." When we all turned to her, she shook her head. "I don't know it first-hand, but there's been talk."

Luke feigned shock. "Talk? Does that mean my boy has a naughty past?" He batted his eyelashes, pulled a bowl of popcorn onto his lap, and pretended to rapt attention while he shoved in the over-buttered kernels. "Dish, darling. Lukey needs to know."

I laughed. "Oh Lord. Give him something or we're going to be listening to third person Luke all night."

## CHAPTER TWENTY-ONE

Since it was my off night, I cleaned the kitchen, cleared out dust bunnies, cobwebs, and all the other stuff that had been neglected lately. Thanks to my new nightly activities I hadn't had much time for cleaning.

I really didn't mind all the distractions. I liked staying busy and didn't love cleaning so much.

The latter was why I was thankful when the phone rang. Cleaning kept my hands busy, but it allowed my mind too much free-range Jax time, and I had to pull that back quickly. Not picture those chameleon eyes of his, or the breadth of his chest, the strength in his hands when he clasped mine.

Thank goodness the phone was persistent so I could snap out of my mind musings. "Hello?"

"Hey, Bond girl. Jordan has a skip he wants you to track. A big one. Says he needs his best team on it." Cleo sounded excited about this one.

The praise shot a bolt of pride through me. We were three for three. About to make it four for four.

"Should I call him, or do you have the info?" If she had a fax, we could go off of, there wouldn't be a need to deal with Jordan's big personality more than after we caught the skip.

"I'll shoot you a screenshot." She hung up.

As far as business managers went, she was aces. I didn't have to worry about anything but catching the skip, and the increase in my bank accounts that she made sure happened.

I dialed Kendra, and she did the tracking spell, so we knew where we were going. I picked her up to drive into the city. The bond price on this woman was a big one, and I wanted to make sure we caught her. Plus, I liked being the team Jordan went to when he needed a skip caught. I didn't want to jeopardize our status.

We drove to the apartment, knocked on the door with a *delivery* for her and she answered. Kendra took her into custody, and I cuffed her while I explained the procedure once we took her in. Easy peasy.

Kendra drove to the station while I sat in the back with the skip. Then, once we picked up our bounty receipt we drove to Jordan's.

"Well, well, well. You guys are like Pippen and Jordan." I wasn't sure of the reference but smiled. My blank look must've demanded clarification because he rolled his eyes and scrubbed his hands over his face. "A dream team? You don't watch basketball?"

Kendra frowned. "Not basketball from the 1980s." She shoved the receipt across the counter. "We prefer Bond Girls, not dream team."

Jordan nodded. "I do love that name." He pulled out the checkbook. "Should I make it out to the Bond Girls or to one of you?"

Cleo had opened our business account after our last payday. "Bond Girls is fine."

Without much more conversation—it was a late night even for Jordan standards—we walked out.

And ran straight into Blake. I was beginning to wonder if he was tracking me.

"Well, hello, beautiful Hailey." He spoke quietly. "I have quite a surprise for you lovely ladies."

I could've done without all the syrupy weirdness. I looked at Kendra. She looked at me. Maybe it was instinct, or maybe his weird vibe, but we mouthed,

"Run!" and as we were about to take off, Blake moved with his speed of light quickness and had his hand on Kendra's throat before I could react.

He lowered his voice. "If you scream, make a single sound, or try to fight, I'll rip her throat out. We both know there's nothing you can do to stop me."

To have that kind of speed, he was obviously old. Obviously strong, too. I nodded.

Blake grinned. "Good, then. We're going to go for a little walk, and you're both going to behave yourselves, or I'll kill you in the street and disappear before your little boyfriend even knows there's a problem. Understand?"

I hated people who needed clarification that I was paying attention. "Of course, I understand." I snapped at him because he might've had the power, but he wanted us alive. Probably needed and I was willing to bet my bad attitude on it.

He took his hand off of Kendra's throat, but kept a firm grip on her arm, although to any passersby, it probably looked normal enough, especially in this neighborhood. I wanted to signal Kendra to let her body go limp, but I couldn't without alerting this jerk face since he'd stationed himself between us.

"What do you want from us?" I asked. "Who are you, really?" But he didn't answer. Instead, he walked us toward a warehouse with enough graffiti and broken windows it looked as if it belonged in some sort of scary movie.

"Shut up and go inside." I did as directed, all the while trying to think of a way out that wouldn't compromise Kendra's safety. Maybe if we got inside, and he let her go, she could do a spell or a chant to subdue him, to at least give me a fighting chance. Or maybe she could summon a coven to help. I didn't know if her powers could do that. I only knew mine were no match for his.

It turned out the graffiti on the walls were runes. My guess was spell dampeners which would keep Kendra from her magical abilities.

"Who the hell are you?" Kendra demanded as he shoved her, and she fell to her knees.

"I'm the guy who compelled your friend Jordan so he would tell me right where you were." Not a stellar feat, since I was pretty sure Jordan was the kind of guy who wouldn't be all too resistant to a good compulsion.

Not many humans could.

"What do you want with us?" My voice came out high-pitched and shrill.

I knelt down beside Kendra to check on her, but

the jerk face lifted me up by my hair. "Stop it!" I screamed.

He cackled a laugh. "You are pathetic and stupid, and I cannot abide such in a member of my race."

Oh, Lord. He was one of those. A zealot. And an idiot. Not a winning combination. And with one flick of his wrist, the glamour that made him gorgeous fell away and he was just an average looking vampire. Nothing to write home about, for sure.

He lifted his arm and backhanded me across the cheek. He knew I couldn't be killed by beating me to death, but I was willing to bet he was going to try.

"Allow me to introduce myself. My name is Kalon. I'm sorry to interrupt your night, but I needed you to lure your little boyfriend here." He jerked my hair again. "Now, I need you to be very scared, very injured so he feels it."

"Why would he feel it?" I wasn't well acquainted yet with my connection to Jax.

"Oh, for goodness' sake. Pathetic *and* stupid." He shook his head and twisted my hair again around his fist. "He's your maker. He can feel all your emotions. Might even be able to read your little mind. So, call for him."

When I didn't flinch, he struck me again. Pain blossomed in my cheek, and I would've fallen if not for the hand in my hair. "Do I need to convince you?"

And he started with a punch to my stomach. After a few punches, Kendra rebounded and jumped on his back.

"How did I not feel your magic?" she grunted, yanking his neck back with both hands under his chin. He threw her off easily without ever letting me go. She crumpled onto the floor.

"I have a very talented witch in my pocket." He grinned, and evil rolled off of him in waves. It was blatant and dark. Chilling in ways I didn't care for. I jerked, trying for freedom, but he held on.

That was when I opened my mind and called out to Jax. I wasn't sure I was doing it right. I hoped so. Because I needed my maker to come and teach Kalon some manners. Or I was going to die here tonight. For real dead.

## CHAPTER TWENTY-TWO

He continued to try to torture me with a couple of kicks to my stomach, a few punches to my jaw, and more than a few times, he pounded my head against the concrete floor. But I was young and healing almost as fast as he inflicted the punishment.

That didn't stop the pain.

Growing frustrated, Kalon went in for the kill, to rip my throat out with the strength in his fingers, but before he got a good grip, an overhead door pushed up and Jax, Ransom and Paige stood at the edge of the loading area.

Kalon let me go, and I fell to the ground as Jax advanced, stalking Kalon with his fangs bared and murder in his eyes. His fists clenched at his side. "Run, Hailey."

But I wasn't going anywhere.

Kendra was against the wall scraping a rune from the concrete, and Ransom went to stand beside her while Paige helped me up and we moved to Kendra's side. "Help me," she hissed.

I scraped with her. She needed the runes gone so she could work a little magic. Help out the good guys.

Jax pounced on Kalon, and they battled, throwing one another into posts that held up the building, rolling on the ground into walls that dented, and crumbling the concrete under their strength. The whole place smelled like a sewer and there was no telling what had been done in here before we arrived, but I was glad for a moment to recover. The punches hadn't done much more than hurt, but they had been powerful. I'd lost a lot of blood in the few minutes Kalon had beaten me.

More vamps poured in through the open doorway—followers of Kalon's who attacked Ransom and Paige while I gave my body a minute to heal before jumping into the fray. I was young in terms of vampire strength, but I'd been training like a prize fighter lately, and there was no way one of these asshats was taking me down.

I punched. Kicked. Sidestepped a biter.

A woman with long robes tied at her waist by a gold cord walked through the room, a whirlwind of energy around her. Papers and debris from the floor swirled in serious tornado action while she walked closer. I wanted to stop her, but I couldn't. I had two vamps taking pot shots at me, and I was in an advance-retreat mode of defense.

In a moment of distraction, I took a hard right cross to the jaw and saw a couple of stars before it cleared. Rage poured through me. Why they were fighting for Kalon, I didn't know, but they were my enemies now, and I had to prove I could handle myself.

I glanced at Kendra. Whoa. She was glowing, levitating a couple of feet above the action and the walking witch struggled, kicking her legs as Kendra pulled her off the ground. Their fight stayed in the air while the vamps fought on the ground. Paige roared while Ransom beat his attackers back with a steel pipe, he wielded like he'd taken batting practice with the majors.

But I kept my body squared where Jax would never be far from my periphery. I wanted to be able to see him. Not that I could do much against a vamp like Kalon, but if Jax fell, I would be there, fighting to the death, no matter what I had to do to get to him.

I worked my way into the corner and to a broom. I broke it over my knee and created two pointed stakes. I jabbed one of my vamps through the heart and stepped back as his body imploded. Now I just had the tattooed vamp he'd brought with him. She was long haired and glassy eyed. When she knelt, distraught, to run her hands through the mess of blood and guts her little friend left behind, I grabbed her by the hair, lifted her chin and staked her. "You got staked." No, that wasn't a good catchphrase. I'd come up with something eventually.

As I ended my vamps, I looked over my shoulder at Jax just in time to watch him rip off Kalon's head. As literally as one could be ripped off by the bare-handed grip of a vampire. Jax threw the open-mouthed skull to the side.

Like they'd been released from a spell, the remaining vamps stopped fighting, stood, and turned to bow to Jax.

Above us, the fight between Kendra and Kalon's witch raged on. Kendra shot a ball of fire, and the witch moved to the side. She sent a bolt of power at Kendra and missed. Kendra advanced, took the other woman by the throat and wrapped the cord from the woman's waist around her neck.

She murmured a few words in Latin and the woman fell, hitting the ground hard.

When Ransom moved to stop her from running out, Kendra called out. "Let her go. I stripped her power."

He stepped aside and the woman limped to the big door before she picked up her robes and ran.

The battle was over. For now.

I stood beside Kendra as Jax and Ransom rolled Kalon's body into one of those blue construction tarps. They loaded him into the back of a van. I didn't ask where it came from, because this was very likely one of those need-to-know situations and after careful consideration, I didn't need to know. I also didn't want to know.

"Why didn't his body explode?" I asked.

"He was too old," Jax replied as he held the door open for me. "He'll slowly crumble."

I sat beside Jax, who told me to stay close while Ransom drove the van and Paige and Kendra brought the Prius to Jax's house. Jax held my hand, stroking my palm with his thumb, but didn't speak. Every once in a while, he glanced at me, but what-ever he might've wanted to say, he kept to himself.

"What're you going to do with his body in the meantime?" My voice sounded small and weak, but it was what I could manage.

"Are you sure you want to know?" Jax asked.

I nodded, not sure at all. "Of course." I said it like I was a badass, but if the answer involved disemboweling or cutting him up for spare parts, or feeding off of him, I was out. So far out it would take a shuttle and a team of astronauts to get to me.

"I have a cremation chamber in the basement," Jax said simply.

I laughed. Maniacal. Disbelieving. "Oh sure. I bet that was a big selling point for the realtor." I laughed a little more. "Black out windows, fully stocked bar, and a dungeon with a cremation chamber. Really drove the price up, I bet."

His voice was calm, soothing, soft. "It's going to be okay, Hailey."

I asked the question I hadn't wanted an answer to before, so I'd never let myself consider it. But now I had to know. "What happens if I don't get the hang of this vampire thing? Am I going to end up in the basement barbecuer?"

He narrowed his eyes. "No, of course not." He ran his finger from my temple to my jaw then around to my chin and lifted so I was looking into his eyes. "I will never hurt you. You're a part of me."

I could've drowned in his eyes, in the sincerity in his voice, in the emotion stirring in my belly. I nodded, and he pulled me to him and kissed the top of my head.

Ten minutes later, Ransom pulled the car around the back of the house, through the fence Jax opened for him and pulled shut when the van was hidden inside. When Ransom parked at the back door, Jax lifted Kalon's body and tossed it over his shoulder in a fireman's carry. The unsecured head rolled out and Ransom picked it up, easy as pie.

I gasped. Kalon's eyes were wide and colorless, his lips parted, fangs dangling now.

"Go on inside. I'll be up in a few minutes." Jax nodded at me as if he was telling me it was all going to be okay, and when he said it, I believed it. Until he walked down the steps to the walkout basement door.

Then the nerves came back, and I stood watching. I just couldn't stop myself from walking down and peeking in the window. Jax opened a metal hatch and pushed the body inside, then hit a button so a fire burst up and lit the tarp. Ransom threw the head in, and they stood for a minute as the skin bubbled, then shut the hatch and turned. I ran up the steps and was inside on the sofa before they made it to the basement door.

Jax came in and sat beside me. "You okay?"

I nodded.

"You don't have to be tough right now. It's just us, and I know I was pretty messed up the first time I saw a body burn." I didn't acknowledge the fact that he knew I'd been watching.

"I'm fine." I wasn't, but I would be so long as he kept touching my hand, soothing me with his soft voice and steady fingers.

"I have to call Dominic and let him know I killed Kalon." He laced his fingers through mine then pulled them back and stared while he slid his palm against mine, back and forth.

"Why do we have to tell?" Good riddance in my book.

"I need to get to Dominic before any of the vamps who had known of Kalon's plan do. Their spin will be a lot harsher than the truth. I'm already on the radar for affecting the vampire population. This will be another strike." He spoke as if he'd done something wrong by killing Kalon.

"Even though you killed him to save us?" Certainly, there had to be some concession for killing one vampire to save three. And a witch. And what about the vampire I killed? Will they hold me responsible for that?

"Yeah." I didn't know if it was his worry I felt as much as I heard or if it worked the other way. I only knew his emotion was palpable. I was swimming in it.

# CHAPTER TWENTY-THREE

It took a couple of days to scrub the sight of Kalon's burning body from my mind. But once I did, I was back to myself as much as I could be during the waking hours. We'd just captured a particularly well-paying skip, so I was in the mood to party.

I called Luke. "Party at my place. Bring your dancing shoes and your iPod. I'll handle everything else."

Luke couldn't resist a good party. "What are we celebrating?"

"Why does it matter?"

He chuckled like I was the dumbest woman he'd ever spoken to. "I need to know whether we're going formal or California casual."

"It's a middle of the night party under the stars. Dress for mosquitoes." I smiled, then hung up and called everyone else.

An hour later, we all stood around with drinks raised. "To the Bond Girls Recovery Agency!" We were officially a company staffed by me, Kendra, and Paige. Cleo said she would work with us, but she wanted her freedom to work when she wanted and vacation when it suited her.

Paige drank her glass of blood like she was throwing back a shot of tequila. "Hell, yeah."

"You already have a job as head of my enforcers." Jax stood beside me, and I absorbed as much of his closeness as I could while he spoke to Paige.

She chuffed out a breath and shook her head. "Oh, ye of little faith. I can do both."

Ransom grinned. "I don't want to be known as a Bond Girl, but I can help out every once in a while, too."

Jax leaned down so his breath was warm on my ear. "You're stealing all of my employees."

Before I could reply, the back gate swung open and Dominic stood staring, bobbing his head as if he was counting before he walked through.

He stood at the edge of our little talking circle and nodded at Jax. "Jaxon. I was sorry to hear about the death of Kalon. Furthermore, I was surprised you left such a dangerous message on my voicemail." Jax didn't react more than to tense his muscles.

Even I could see there was more coming. I motioned for Luke to go inside and compelled it with my mind. If some supernatural punishment was coming, I didn't need my brother to see it. He walked inside as Dominic continued. "The elders demand your presence." He paused. "There is much for you to answer for."

"Who?" I had to ask in some slim chance he wasn't talking to me.

"All of you." When I turned, he tapped my shoulder. "It's time for you to meet the elders and be justified."

WE HOPED you enjoyed Bitten in the Midlife. Find out what is in store for Hailey and her friends in the next installment of Fanged After Forty, Staked in the Midlife.

## FANGED AFTER FORTY

Fanged After Forty is a new witty spin-off from the bestselling series Witching After Forty about a forty year old nurse who moves to Philly after being left at the alter on her wedding day. The move and fresh start becomes more than Hailey Whitfield bargained for.

Now she is forty and fanged and took on a new career, Bounty Hunting.

### Reading Order:
Bitten in the Midlife
Staked in the Midlife
Masquerading in the Midlife
Many more adventures to come...

## WITCHING AFTER FORTY SERIES

Witching After Forty follows the misadventures of Ava Harper – a forty-something necromancer with a light witchy side that you wouldn't expect from someone who can raise the dead. Join Ava as she learns how to start over after losing the love of her life, in this new paranormal women's fiction series with a touch of cozy mystery, magic, and a whole lot of mayhem.

A Ghoulish Midlife
Cookies for Satan (Christmas novella)
I'm With Cupid (Valentine novella)
A Cursed Midlife
Feeding Them Won't Make Them Grow (Novella in the Charity Anthology, Eat Your Heart Out)

A Girlfriend For Mr. Snoozerton (Novella)
A Haunting Midlife
An Animated Midlife
A Killer Midlife
More coming soon

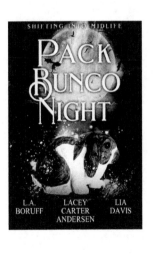

**A bunny bit me on the finger and everything went sideways after that.**

That's just the beginning of my insane life. The Fascinators, the local ladies' club, suddenly are incredibly interested in having me join their next Bunco night, which is a thinly veiled excuse to drink and gossip.

I've been dying to get into that group for years; why now? I'm over forty, my daughter is grown, and all I do is temp work. What's so special about me?

After I shift into a dragon, things become clearer. They're not a Bunco group. The Fascinators are a pack of shifters. Yes, shifters. Like werewolves, except in this case it's weresquirrels and a wereskunk, among others.

And my daughter? She wants to move home, suddenly and suspiciously. As excited as I am to have her home, why? She loves being on her own. It's got something to do with a rough pack of predators, shifters who want to watch the world burn. I hope she's not mixed up with the wrong crowd.

There's also a mysterious mountain man hanging around out of the blue. Where was he before the strange bunny bite? Nowhere near me, that's for sure.

Life is anything but boring. At this point, I'm just hoping that I'll survive it all with my tail—literally —intact.

Preorder your copy today

## Magical Midlife in Mystic Hollow https://
laboruff.com/books/mystic-hollow/

*Karma's Spell*

*Karma's Shift*

*Karma's Spirit*

## Girdles & Ghouls, A Halloween PWF

## Anthology http://www.books2read.com/girdles

Find more books by Lia Davis here:

https://authorliadavis.com/

Find more books by L.A. Boruff here: www.

laboruff.com

Follow the authors' social media!

Lia's Facebook

L.A.'s Facebook

Lia's Insta

L.A.'s Insta

Alfred's Insta

Lia's Bookbub

L.A.'s Bookbub

Lia's Amazon

L.A.'s Amazon

## ABOUT LIA DAVIS

Lia Davis is the USA Today bestselling author of more than forty books, including her fan favorite Shifter of Ashwood Falls Series.

A lifelong fan of magic, mystery, romance and adventure, Lia's novels feature compassionate alpha heroes and strong leading ladies, plenty of heat, and happily-ever-afters.

Lia makes her home in Northeast Florida where she battles hurricanes and humidity like one of her heroines.

When she's not writing, she loves to spend time with her family, travel, read, enjoy nature, and spoil her kitties.

She also loves to hear from her readers. Send her a note at lia@authorliadavis.com!

*Follow Lia on Social Media*

Website: http://www.authorliadavis.com/

Newsletter: http://www.
subscribepage.com/authorliadavis.newsletter
Facebook author fan page: https://www.
facebook.com/novelsbylia/
Facebook Fan Club: https://www.facebook.com/
groups/LiaDavisFanClub/
Twitter: https://twitter.com/novelsbylia
Instagram: https://www.
instagram.com/authorliadavis/
BookBub: https://www.bookbub.com/authors/lia-
davis
Pinterest: http://www.pinterest.com/liadavis35/
Goodreads: http://www.goodreads.com/author/
show/5829989.Lia_Davis

L.A. (Lainie) Boruff lives in East Tennessee with her husband, three children, and an ever growing number of cats. She loves reading, watching TV, and procrastinating by browsing Facebook. L.A.'s passions include vampires, food, and listening to heavy metal music. She once won a Harry Potter trivia contest based on the books and lost one based on the movies. She has two bands on her bucket list that she still hasn't seen: AC/DC and Alice Cooper. Feel free to send tickets.

L.A.'s Facebook Group: https://www.facebook.com/groups/LABoruffCrew/

Follow L.A. on Bookbub if you like to know about

new releases but don't like to be spammed: https://
www.bookbub.com/profile/l-a-boruff

Printed in Great Britain
by Amazon

17674009R00159